Dear Ir...

    Wish...

Con mucho gusto,

            Fred Hoctor
            Campoleco
            1992

    Did all this stuff really happen? I don't know. I
guess so.
    I don't remember.

Cover illustration by Darrel Millsap, San Diego
Design by Tom Lewis, The Design Quarter, San Diego
Illustration and logo copyright © 1984 by Fred Hoctor

14 of the 26 stories in this book originally appeared in full or abbreviated form in
Hoctor's column "Baja Inside Out" in the *Baja Times* between May,1982 and
November, 1983, under the editorship, first, of Roberta Ridgely and,
from June, 1983, Carlos Chabert. Part of "My Mother the Doctor" also
appeared in the *Mexico West Newsletter* during that period.

ISBN 0-915855-00-3

Library of Congress Catalog Number 83-73602

First Edition, April, 1984. Printed in the U.S.A.

This is a very best effort by

BACKSIDE PRESS
A MARK OF DESPERATION

P.O. Box 112412, San Diego, CA 92111-0220

E Pluribus Unum

To Sylvia

AUTHOR'S NOTE

A few characters are composites. I have not always described them or quoted them accurately, and I have altered and invented a few scenes for continuity, but for the most part, yeah, this is the way it happened.

AUTHOR'S THANKS

To Roberta Ridgely for white-hot encouragement and a bold, blue pencil; to the folks at CompuText for wordprocessing/typesetting/editing magic and invaluable suggestions; to Neil Morgan who proved again what a nice human being he is; to Bob Cary for his professorial expertise; to Darrel Millsap for his illustrating genius and to Tom Lewis for his captivating jacket design and cherished friendship and to the whole Baja Haha gang. *Salud!*

CONTENTS

PROLOGUE — MEXICO'S PAINTED LADY . . .   7
WILDEST SALOON IN THE WEST 13
THE MOVEABLE FEAST 21
THE BIG PIGEON CAPER 26
BEST LITTLE WHOREHOUSE IN BAJA 33
THE MAGIC MUSHROOMS 38
PAPPY O'TOOLE, VAUDEVILLIAN 47
MY MOTHER THE DOCTOR 65
THE LAST LAUGH 77
THE HAIRCUT PLACE 81
THE HAPPINESS BOYS 86
FAMOUS ANIMALS I HAVE KNOWN 93
'TIL DEATH DO US PART 101
WATSON COME HERE, I NEED YOU 105
FASTEST GUN IN THE WEST 113
THE YULE FROG 120
THE MAN BEHIND THE FROG 125
AMOK IN A MEXICAN BAKERY 135
MAÑANA 143
THE HAMBURGER THAT GOBBLED 150
FLY NOW, PRAY LATER 161
THE GRINGO CURSE 168
THE TOYMAN 176
HOW BIG *WAS* THAT FISH, JOHNNY? 182
COMING OF AGE IN BAJA 190
WANNA BUY A DUCK? 197
MOBY DUCK 209

MEXICO'S PAINTED LADY

What the hell is this book all about?

Funny you should ask.

I was kind of hoping for a *Gone With The Wind*, or something maybe less elegant but more literate, in the style, let's see... of a Saul Bellow or a Kurt Vonnegut, but what came out was a goofy bedside primer of tales about some of the wonderful people and whackos I've met while stumbling around for 30 years in the big sandbox called "Baja."

Among others, you'll meet a dotty, buxom Brünnhilde who bullwhips beer cans every morning and has a way with turkeys; a phantom artist who paints boulders to look like frogs; a fierce Seri Indian who plays a strange chess game with wooden ducks as pawns; plus a glamorous old medicine woman who once drank me under the table and who to this day cures my occasional headaches by brewing a special tea made from purple bougainvillea bracts. One of the characters isn't even human — it's Kojak, the famous dancing pig of Campo Loco.

Like the phone book, there are lots of characters, but not much of a plot.

I am bonkers about Baja and her gentle people, and about all the fruitcakes, hippy-dips, comedians, con men, preachers and pirates who have passed this way in my lifetime. I just thought I had better get some of them on paper before my memory fades and I get so old I have to browbeat a sawbones to take a tuck in my wattle.

There is something about Baja that attracts exotic characters. Last week I ran into a retired Air Force sergeant who was living on top of a mountain, in the middle of nowhere, with his bride and a gabby 95-year-old mother-in-law. He was busy with a pick and shovel, building a nine-hole "golf course" out in the remote desert chaparral, and he was furious because the cups kept getting filled up with rattlers. He couldn't get the flags to stand up straight. The old woman shook my cage for two hours, explaining to me how Maximilian, the Emperor of Mexico, had somehow escaped the firing squad at the Hill of the Bells and had come to live with her family in South Texas when she was just a little girl. "Uncle Max" I think she called him.

Quien sabe?

After spending some time in Baja, one begins to think nothing of the outrageous qualities of characters like this, because going fruitloops seems to be a way of life down here.   I am not the world's most well-adjusted guy myself. I have trouble remembering my name and my watch only ticks

8

every four seconds. Much of my problem, as you will see, stems from hanging around down here.

The chief character is Baja herself, a rambunctious old hooker who wears lots of paint and wiggles her buns at almost everybody she meets.

I once told an editor-type in New York that I was thinking of doing a book about Baja, and when she stopped laughing she wondered aloud about what possible reader interest there could be in a doubtfully humorous volume concerning a dirt racetrack somewhere south of Los Angeles. Most Californians are familiar with Baja, but the vast majority of *Norte Americanos* seem to think of the place as Parnelli Jones' playground and nothing more. This, of course, is because of the world-wide publicity surrounding the famous Baja 1000 off-road race and an occasional T-V commercial showing a hot pickup bouncing along over Baja's Vizcaino desert. But Baja is certainly more than just a bunch of bumpy roads.

More than 37 million people (including Mexicans) cross the Baja border at Tijuana every year, making it the busiest border crossing in the world, and at least five major Baja cities thrive on tourism. With 17 million gawkers annually, Baja now draws five times more tourists than Hawaii.

Why we *gringos** overlooked Baja when we stole

_____

* I have used the word *gringo* in this book with none of its sometimes-hostile overtones. Here it simply means "foreigners."

the rest of California from the Mexicans, I will never know. Baja is a class-A piece of real estate — 690 miles long, 187 miles across in one place, 53,000 square miles. If you wanted to, you could squeeze 43 Rhode Islands in here, but it would be a terrible shame.

While Tijuana, a city of 1½ million people, has lots of hustle and bustle and has been influenced slightly by the 20th Century, most of Baja is a lot like what we read of the American Southwest in the 1880s, and life is pretty much as it was then. There are still cowboys and Indians, *bandidos*, big ranches, saloons, sheriffs on horseback, dance hall girls and all that. Baja is in a time warp. An anachronistic frontier attitude pervades the place.

In fact, the locals aptly call Northern Baja "La Frontera," or "The Frontier" (explaining the abbreviation "FRONT" on *Baja Norte* license plates), and you'd better be ready for anything when you pass through them swingin' doors at the border, podner. Now. About the painted lady herself.

First of all, she is not properly called "Baja," but "Baja California," meaning "Lower California." I realize that "Lower" is a strange nickname for a chunk of territory where a healthy portion of the populace is high most of the time, but that's the way things are.

Baja California is a peninsula. It is longer than Italy and nearly twice the size of Ireland. On one side is the gorgeous Gulf of California, otherwise known as the "Sea of Cortez." (It is not the Gulf of

Mexico. That is another puddle entirely.) On the other side is the Pacific Ocean. There are a couple of respectable humps down the middle of the place, sierras where it snows in the winter, and there are a few jungle-like oases surrounding the occasional water holes, but other than that the peninsula is largely sand, savage desert mountains and giant Hopalong Cassidy boulders. In some places the back roads are covered with fine silt about a foot deep. The stuff is like talcum powder and you can get lost in it. In other places the landscape is strewn with metamorphic rock shards that will carve a new set of treads in your Michelins.

Cold? How cold *is* Baja, Johnny? Well, I'll tell you, Ed. It's so-o-o cold that the winter wind, coming off the mountain snows, will nip your little tushy right through your L. L. Bean arctic sleeping bag. Yet, in the summer, the thermometer can yo-yo around the 120 mark. It gets so hot, you can drink a case of Baja's famous Triple-X beer and pee dust.

The beginnings of Baja are murky. Some itinerant redskins came through here about two or three thousand years ago and left some spectacular graphics on the walls of caves in the South-Central part of the peninsula, but the pictures don't tell us much about the price of frijoles at the time, or where one caught the trolley for San Diego.

For at least the last four centuries, people of many nationalities have tried to tame Baja. They're a motley bunch — English, Germans, French, Dutch, Chinese, Russians, gringo tourists and, of course,

11

the Mexicans. The Mexicans won, more or less, but remnants of the other cultures are everywhere in Baja. Gene Carrasco, a Baja P. R. man, once advised me with a straight face that the "national" food of Baja is egg foo yung.

Why does Baja have such allure for blithe spirits? Why do even the most rational gringos seem to go mentally mushy when they get here? How do the native Bajans (relatively sane and sober, yet a colorful lot themselves) react to the "gringo curse"? If ye seek in these pages, ye shall find.

An important tip: I have found that this book makes just as much sense if you read it backwards.

—   Fred Hoctor
        Campo Loco
        Baja California, 1984

WILDEST SALOON IN THE WEST

When I was a kid, just starting out in the business of writing for a living, I used to hang out in bars because a) I became terrifically intelligent when drinking and b) I got some of my best material in bars. I picked good saloons: The Men's Pub in Boston, where the late comedian Billy de Wolfe hung out; Sardi's in midtown New York; and a dump called Nick's in Greenwich Village. Oh yeah, and the old Press Club in Los Angeles. Strange things happened in these places.

But I was a babe in the woods until I plopped down on a barstool in Baja's now-famous Hussong's cantina in the '50s. The place was only a few hours south of San Diego, along the coast and through the mountains. A lot of people at the ad agency where I worked had talked about it. For some reason I pictured the place as a quiet little watering hole where one could have a pleasant drink or two and sample the charms of "Old Mexico." I was wrong.

Comedian Phil Harris was tending bar and selling autographs for a peso. Some sparsely clad cream-puff from San Francisco did an inchworm act the length of the long bar. And a guy, who probably never handled more than a six-foot dinghy, swash-buckled in wearing a sword and an eye patch and regaled everybody with his plan to take Ensenada Harbor for "Jolly Old King George," whoever that was.

I was astonished at silver-haired Percy Hussong's blasé attitude about these shenanigans until he un-loaded his considered opinion on me. "They're just drunk," he said sullenly, and retired to the back room to get away from the noise.

The famous cantina in Ensenada, 60 miles down the peninsula, is one of the last of the truly authentic old-time saloons in the West, and it's a rip-roarer.

It was founded at the end of the last century by a German immigrant when the population of the town was less than 5000 souls (population now exceeds 180,000) and it has changed very little over the years, from the turn-of-the-century wooden facade ("Hussong's Cantina - Fundada 1892") to the saw-dust on the floors.

The ceilings are of coffered tin; the large fire-place, around which thousands of *mariachis* (musi-cians) have played over the years, still stands; and the famous long bar and rough-carpentered back bar are still intact.

A friend once described the architecture to me as "early Baja sleaze." The standing aroma has always

14

been a mixture of Pine Sol and sour tequila.

Hussong's is, and always was, a place where anything can happen. I once saw a laid-back San Diego businessman walk into the place on a hot July evening, dressed in a Santa Claus outfit, playing *When The Saints Go Marching In* on a crumpled school-band tuba. The crowd barely acknowledged his presence.

Up until recent years, most of Ensenada's tourist business (and much of its official business) was planned from the back office at Hussong's.

The city fathers often gathered in Percy's office for decision-making and consultation with the old man, and high-stake poker was not unknown.

Old Percy sat behind the clutterless desk with a single old-fashioned telephone and played Judge Roy Bean. He was a tough little guy with piercing blue eyes and very fair skin. His smiles were rare, but everyone seemed to love him. From the antique safe, he lent thousands of dollars on faith to unknown gringos for "gettin' home" money. He was a one-man chamber of commerce and information bureau. And he dispensed frontier justice pretty much as he saw fit, meting out tough sentences when the crime was sufficient. He had no patience with brawlers, especially, and with one wave of his hand a troop of police would pounce on the offenders and cart them off to the *carcel* (jail). One time, though, a particularly young offender was brought to him in the back office. Knowing the rough treatment the boy might get in the jail, Percy thought

15

twice about banishing him to the dungeon.

"Drive him to the edge of town," he said to the cop who was holding the boy. "And see that he keeps going." The kid is now grown tall and is a successful Denver artist who contributes a very decent sum annually to an Ensenada orphanage of my acquaintance. The check is always made out in the name of Percy Hussong.

When Percy died in the early '70s at San Diego's Scripps Hospital, relatives took over and decided to "modernize" by giving the cantina a coat of paint, during which many of the artifacts, historical pictures and caricatures of the old timers were stolen or "disappeared." But the trophy head of the great horned kudu, a relic of a Hussong safari (though it looks like an overstuffed moose) still hangs on the wall near the back office.* Percy's old oak school desk and safe are still back there. And some of the Hussong international-paper-money collection is still mounted on the back bar.

The Indian lady with the basket of tamales on her head is gone. The crippled kid, who used to push himself around the sawdust on a skateboard-like contraption, long ago was treated to a stateside operation after a pass-the-hat session by the "regulars," and can now be seen only occasionally, belly up

---

* I don't really know if it is a great horned kudu. However it is *one* of those crossword puzzle animals, maybe an eland. I am just enamored of the euphony of "great horned kudu."

16

to the bar. I haven't seen the *cacahuate* (peanut) vendor for a long time, and a lot of the old bartenders have vanished. But the costume-jewelry peddlers still roam around, the caricaturist (though tired of it all) is still on duty, and the mariachis still belt out *La Bamba* at regular intervals, thus revving up the action, but now charging exorbitant fees for their music.

The strange thing about Hussong's is that it is the only saloon in all of Mexico (that I know of) which has remained a haunt, since the beginning, of both gringos and Mexicanos without being taken over totally by one or the other. Albeit there is still a pervasive aloofness in the air, countless Anglo-Mexican friendships have been sealed here, and the joint has always outdistanced Berlitz as a language school. (Most gringos speak worse Spanish, and most Bajans better English than they let on, I have found.)

On the weekend of the Newport-to-Ensenada race — it is unofficially called the "enchilada derby" and is the largest yacht race in the world — and during the Baja off-road races, the paddy wagon literally shuttles between the cantina and the pokey. Arrests exceed a couple dozen on a good weekend, for activities ranging from cocaine possession and aggravated assault to indecent exposure or watering the dust in the parking lot. Because the dump is always crawling with cops, both in uniform and plain clothes, and the windows are boarded up during busy weekends, brawlers seldom do a lot of damage before the cuffs are slapped on, though they are often egged on by the crowd, who think of themselves as stuntmen in a B western.

The new-breed Hollywood people who now visit Hussong's wear Beverly Hills western boots and Gucci accessories and call each other "Sweety." And a chubby old mariachi sings an hilarious dis-syncopated version of *Way Down South In the Land Of Cotton* in Spanglish — the hip, slick and cool kids don't know any Mexican songs and are forever requesting something they can "relate to."

During midweek, when the tourists have gone, a few of the old habitués return when the doors open at 10 a.m., but the marathon chess games, the ubiquitous decks of cards, the resounding clack of the dominoes as they are slapped on the table Baja-style, the philosophizing and tale-telling are mostly a thing of the past. Most of the great liars are dead, and their livers are at Johns Hopkins.

Some of the youngsters from the new colleges in Ensenada sometimes congregate in the cantina to celebrate a birthday or the end of finals, or just to see what the gringos are up to, but drink prices are steep now, and like students everywhere they usually do their serious drinking on more affordable turf.

The place is never boring. There are always a few cowboys, round-the-world sailors, soldiers of fortune, etc.

"My God," a naive tourist once said to me after sipping one of Hussong's insidious Margaritas, "if they fixed this place up, it would make a fortune!"

Ho and another ho.

The fact is, as grubby as Hussong's is, it has always been one of the world's most profitable saloons. On most summer weekends, especially, hundreds of celebrants squeeze into the 30' by 60' room, glasses are passed overhead from one end of the room to the other and, because of the stiff drinks, customer turnover is spectacular. From 10 a.m. to 4 a.m., literally thousands of guzzlers may pass through, dropping substantial cash in the frenzy of the action.

The recent fad of bumper stickers and T-shirts has only served to make Hussong's even more famous throughout the Southwest. Hussong's is Baja's Gilley's, except that at Hussong's one gets the feeling the bull might come through the door at any moment, and it will *not* be mechanical. Furthermore, capes will appear.

How much is Hussong's worth?

There is no price. It is a gold mine with an endless seam. To a well-heeled collector, the back bar alone might be worth $50,000, if it were for sale. It is intrinsically a worthless piece of wood, roughly assembled. But it *is* from Hussong's.

And the Herculean kudu head on the wall, cracking and torn, might possibly adorn a fancy private bar in Beverly Hills at a similar price — the ultimate whimsy item. But the value of the fixtures is eclipsed by the certain promise of eternal revenue.

Hussong's is the Long Branch, the Crystal Palace and the Silver Dollar all rolled into one, except that Hussong's is still doing business today almost the way it was nearly a century ago. Barring deaths in the family, Hussong's has never been closed.

Robert Coogan (Jackie "The Kid's" brother) once summed up the lure of the larger-than-life bistro succinctly for me as we sat at a back table. "Let's face it," he said, surveying the Mexican cowboy collapsed in a corner, the ball-bearinged blonde doing a strip-tease on a tabletop and the raving hippie being dragged out by a cop, "the joint has class."

The same might be said of *all* of Baja.

THE MOVEABLE FEAST

Since my first trip to Hussong's, I have spent three decades travelling the length and breadth of this amazing peninsula.

There are certain kinds of people in Baja one does not meet in, say, the First Lutheran Church of Toledo, Ohio.

Item: If you are lost in the desert south of San Felipe, you will possibly locate Lena, a barrel-shaped Cocopah Indian who smokes the remains of a charred Kaywoodie pipe which she lights from a portable propane blowtorch. Lena is not there in the winter, but the rest of the year she positions an ancient Servel gas refrigerator and a 25-gallon butane tank wherever she thinks the sparse desert traffic will support sufficient beer sales to make the day worthwhile. There are no signs. No building. No flashing neon. Just Lena and her refrigerator full of ice-cold Carta Blanca, out there among the ocotillo.

When the temperature tops 100, she is an angel of mercy. I have talked to Hollywood actors, ships' captains, renowned authors and fascinating drop-outs who have paused at Lena's sand washes. Lena holds court like a gritty Gertrude Stein, nodding at sage remarks, smiling at witticisms and hugging those of whom she feels particularly fond. She is always an intrinsic part of the proceedings.

Once, at Lena's refrigerator, I got involved in a plethora of palaver with a geology professor from a California university who had an overwhelming need to describe to the assemblage the geological history of the oddly patterned desert mountain range in the distance.

The pedant harangued us non-stop for half an hour, pausing only now and then to down another bottle of suds.

Through it all, Lena reacted with the greatest interest, giggling at bon mots, appearing most concerned at points of serious contention. When it was all over, and the group had roared off in their dune buggies, I approached her quizzically in her native language.

"Lena, I thought you didn't speak English," I ventured. "I had a lot of trouble following that hombre myself. You understood it all?"

She exploded with laughter.

"I don't understand English, amigo," she punctuated with a wink. "Not a word of it. I am just very good at selling beer."

Item: There is a pixieish ex-vaudevillian named

22

Pappy O'Toole, an octogenarian wisp of a gringo, who lives in an Airstream trailer near a bus stop south of Ensenada. He makes the best vodka this side of Murmansk. He'll fill your jug out of a big Sparkletts bottle, *al vibora* (with rattlesnake), and if you stay too long he will play *Moon Over Miami* on the ukelele, do "Cohen on the Telephone" and name every performer on every bill at the Palace from 1922 to 1931. Then he goes to sleep.

Item: There is a portly, moustachioed cantina keeper near San Quintin who is notorious for shooting up his own place on Saturday nights. After he puts the pistola away, he warbles a not-bad imitation of Pavarotti's *Finiculi, Finicula* with an aging dolorous basset hound that howls contrapuntal baritone. The guy spends Sundays patching the .45 holes in the ceiling and spraying the dog's throat with a fine mist of creme de menthe. The liqueur, he claims, improves the animal's tremolo and increases its range by half an octave.

Item: There is a travelling-circus of a man whom the gringos in Baja know only as "Roberto." The Mexicans call him "*El Hombre de Musica*" — The Music Man. He is a mountainous guy topped by flaming red hair, a *Norte Americano* with a Mexican soul, who is liable to be found anywhere on the peninsula because he goes wherever the best fishing happens to be. Roberto learned a full repertoire of traditional old Mexican ranch songs on the concertina while doing a stint in the Hermosillo jail as a callow youth, and he knows all the words. I have seen barbershop quartets of *campesinos* (country people) appear from nowhere when Roberto starts playing that concertina. Once we were camped out on the barren desert on a still night, 20 miles from San Borja. For miles around, the moonscape was so desolate that even the ants were lonesome. At the first squeeze of the box, 33 Mexicans magically appeared from behind the rocks. Nobody went back to work for three days.

Before he starts one of his impromptu gigs, he always pops an inch-long ventriloquial harmonica into his mouth. Folks think it is just a wad of chewing tobacco.

Sometimes he will have to wait an hour or more for a lull in his concertina-playing to coincide with a gap in conversation, at which point he will juggle the harmonica to the forward part of his mouth (yet still out of sight) and launch into a thin and reedy Irish reel.

The trick mystifies everyone, and I have seen people cock their heads at a nearby rock to determine if the tune somehow emanates from its crystalline interior.

Item: I cannot forget Indian Jim, a middle-aged Seminole alligator wrestler from Tampa who "retired" after a self-confessed bank-examiner scam in Baton Rouge and who now spends his days either picking at the bottom of a potentially collapsible turquoise mine, or fishing miles out in the shark-infested Gulf from a flimsy styrofoam canoe.

He fries the fish in a 1948 Studebaker hub cap,

and Roberto aptly remarked that the interior of the old Baptist school bus Jim lives in looks remarkably like Dante's *Inferno*.

Item: Then, of course, there were the Koalani brothers, two Tahitian nightclub performers from Los Angeles who somehow edged their trailer into a narrow mountain pass in Calamajue Canyon and "turned on" for three months. The trailer was equipped with a big Bose sound system, and every night they would give recorded Tahitian-music concerts to the coyotes at full volume and set each other's shirts on fire.

That should give you some idea of the people you are likely to run into down here in Baja.

Of course, if you get *real* lucky, you might cross the path of "The Reverend."

Ah-h-h.

The Reverend.

A fine fellow, he.

A fine fellow.

THE REVEREND T.J. SMITH
AND THE BIG PIGEON CAPER

Among all the kooks in Baja, few ever surpassed the Reverend T. J. Smith in the flamboyance department. (I use a pseudonym for the Reverend here because, though the statute of limitations has run out on many of his escapades, there is still a faint possibility of incarceration.)

T. J. is a ruddy-faced guy with a shock of gray-blond hair and a big silver belt buckle that tilts outward at the base of his paunch. He is one of that vanishing tribe of westerners festooned with big chunks of turquoise (though T.J.'s are of questionable authenticity) and whose spindly legs are set permanently in the gentle angles of a horse's flanks. He smiles always, and calls everybody "Hoss." Wimps love him because he is a legendary figure and he makes them feel like one of the guys.

An erstwhile Arizonan, T. J. drove to the end of a remote Baja road in 1951, the year I discovered him, and found enough Mexicans behind the cacti to build him a cantina. He spent the next twenty years drinking up the profits with the constabulary from a nearby village, who would drive out from town every now and then, supposedly to ask him for his non-existent license and citizenship papers, but more realistically to collect their *mordida*, or "little bite," for allowing him to stay in business.

T. J.'s cantina offered the only steady employment in the area for half a dozen *campesinos*. Nobody was about to run him off.

The cantina was a spectacular hodgepodge of slapdash carpentry and afterthought. The bar was lengthened every year by nailing on another orange crate and talking the Ensenada beer distributor out of one more folding chair.

In the center of the spacious kerosene-lamped barroom was a large oil drum, rigged out with a hole in the front of it and a stove pipe rising to an oversized aperture in the ceiling. On a cold night, T. J. would stuff manzanita roots into the makeshift fireplace until the contraption glowed like a Bessemer furnace.

The floors were dirt, of course, but there were a few old whale bones on the wall ("...to make the place *chick*," T.J. told me).

Some times of the year were pretty slim for T. J., and he hit on a plan to make a few extra bucks. He went up to San Diego, had some fancy marriage licenses printed, and designated himself a member of the cloth. Then he designed a wedding ceremony which began by dusting off the "bride and groom" with a feather duster. "Cleanliness is rat thar next to Godliness," he always explained solemnly to the wedding party. He read the "proceedin's" from a fat hardcover reference volume entitled *The Mechanic's Handbook*. The ceremony was usually just a long string of numbers and formulas, but he guaranteed the marriage would "take." An agate line at the bottom of each license promised "This here marriage good for at least eight hours." For two more bucks he would rent the newlyweds a minuscule "motel room" he had built nearby out of adobe and empty wooden beer-bottle cartons.

T. J. specialized in tall tales which fell just close enough to the realm of believability to be swallowed by middlewesterners who were fascinated with the ocean scenery. Sea foam became "whale eggs." And pointing to the offshore rocks, white with guano, T. J. would gladly take time out from his busy schedule to explain how the tourism department sent "a passel of Messicans out thar every Sunday mornin' to paint them rocks. Look real good, don't they?"

Of course, T. J.'s arms weren't long enough to describe the size of the fish he claimed he caught. Apparently at will. "Get 'em on green chiles," he would say. "Or sometimes garbanza beans. Depends on the time of the year."

T. J. had a famous telephone that was a real

moneymaker. Tourists would come into the cantina and drop dime after dime into it until they finally realized that it wasn't working. "Not working?" he would say. "Well, dang, Hoss. You just keep sluggin' dimes in there and perty soon we'll have the money to buy the wire we need to stretch clear to San Diego. It'll take about a hunnert miles of it, I 'spect." Then he would buy them a beer and leave them laughing.

He had a small cubicle underneath the cantina where he stored block ice. He called it "the sittin' room." Curmudgeons who got nasty on a Saturday night were locked in there for a couple of hours to cool off.

One Sunday afternoon I was quaffing a Carta Blanca with T. J. and taking the sun on the cantina patio.

"What happened to that guy last night who started the fight with the broken beer bottle?" I asked.

T. J. snapped his fingers. "Dang, Hoss, thanks fer remindin' me," he said, and headed for the icehouse door. A shivering tough guy from L. A. emerged terrified, jumped in his car, and was never heard from again.

Another day T. J. came to me with a farming scheme. "Gollee-e-e, Hoss," he said, "we're gonna get rich! I jes' found out them pigs'll eat cactus. And you know how many cactus they is in Baja? Why, it's sure-fire!" I declined the partnership offer, but T. J. leased a patch of cactus up in the mountains and turned a bunch of porkers loose.

There are still pigs roaming somewhere in those mountains and T. J. is not a penny richer. He never figured out how to round the critters up.

Sunday morning was hangover time at T. J.'s and a rotund mother-of-twelve named Anita would cook up a pot of *menudo* (tripe soup) for those who had the energy to show up. Menudo is supposed to mend bones and cure hangovers.

One Sunday no one showed, and T. J. got all upset.

"Dang," he whimpered while waiting for the steamy medicine, "How we ever gonna git an 'A' card lessin we git some customers to try that thar soup?"

Just about that time a flight of handsome white pigeons landed on the sun deck and T. J. squinted at them through the open door.

"Y'like squab, Hoss?" he said, going for his shot-gun in the back room. "Them fellers that was here last night shore might be impressed with a squab dinner."

With that he ground sluiced nine of the birds with a single blast, then grinned in triumph.

"Now, Hoss," he said very seriously, "I got me a lot to do roun' here an' the menudo ain't done yet. Why don't you take them pigeons over thar to the barranca an' give 'em a good pluckin'?"

Never having dismantled a pigeon, I thought it would be a simple task, so I headed for the canyon.

Now, you should know that the owner of these particular fowl was a feisty little Mexican named

Juan Espinoza, from the next sand dune over, who unbeknownst to me had been raising these birds as breeding stock.

As I plucked the white feathers they blew on a gentle wind directly over the hill and landed in his front yard.

It was not long before Juan was standing over me with a pistola, held in a hand seemingly attached to a Norelco vibrator.

Juan's eyes were ablaze.

"Señor," he barked, "I know that you did not do this thing. I warned that *cabron* (S.O.B.) T. J. that if he even *looked* at one of my pigeons I would kill him. Where is he?"

"Back in the cantina," I said shakily, pushing the pile of plucked birds toward him tenderly.

He ignored the offering and started off toward the cantina.

Later, when I had gathered my wits and the scrawny pigeon carcasses, I entered the cantina expecting to find T. J. expired.

He was busily slurping menudo.

"Why the hell didn't you tell me these were Espinoza's birds?" I growled.

"Didn't know," T. J. lied. "Got birds comin' through here all the time. Lotsa birds. Alla time. Feller almost shot me, though. Only thing saved me was the menudo. Old Juan's a downright sucker for menudo. No sense in gittin' him any madder, though."

Then he picked up a sign he had carefully lettered on the gummy end-label from a tomato box with an old lipstick he had found in the restroom. He taped it neatly to the big window in front. I had to go outside to read it:

WHY MAKE MOM COOK?
CHICKEN TONIGHT!

Old T. J. finally got evicted from the cantina when he ran a tent revival at nearby La Bocana and got caught selling watered Wild Turkey to those upon whom he had laid his healing hands. I have heard that he is now operating some kind of a faro game over Mexicali way.

I sorely miss him. He is one of the great rascals of Baja, and a bright red thread in the tapestry.

BEST LITTLE WHOREHOUSE IN BAJA

Not a few ignoble churls have had the temerity to suggest that my accounts of Baja fall fractionally short of being classifiable as history. They are more to be pitied than censured. The fact is, I have chosen more the dimly lit scenes of my Baja past for this book than the big klieg-lighted numbers because I fancy neither marital apocalypse nor extradition from Baja by the authorities.

Anyone who cannot see incidents of humorous grandeur (similar to these I have documented) on any given day in Baja is, to my way of thinking, without powers of observation and should opt for lobotomy before the condition gets too far.

One oaf went so far as to hint that I *exaggerate*, being more concerned with verbal legerdemain than with accuracy. To him I say that I have always reported with the utmost caution, erring — is that possible? — only on the side of conservatism.

I will tell you now about the most famous madame in Baja history, Sixto Rosie Avila, who these days

33

runs a prosperous melon ranch over Tucson way, who long ago compromised the judicial system of Mexicali with a *paso doble* that was simultaneously touching and tragic, and who had a trademark to rival Colette's famous red panties.

Sixto is normally a masculine name, sometimes given by uncreative parents — is *that* possible? — to the sixth boy in the family, so for many years I wondered that Sixto Rosie, with such curves and capacious bodice, should be saddled with the moniker. I only learned after inquiring of an onion trucker from Durango that *Sixto* was the name the gringos had given her, ostensibly because it was thought that she had *six toes*.

In any event, Sixto Rosie's trademark was a pair of bright red woolen socks which she wore, it is said, through thick and thin, and which she waved fiercely in the air during moments of extreme unction.

The socks were, the gringos deduced, to hide her notorious deformity, though whether such natal prolificacy was a reality or no is still (in *my* mind) a matter of some doubt, knowing as I do the average hooker's bent for stage gimmicks. No one will ever know the truth about Rosie's impedimentum, I suspect, except perhaps for a few honeydew pickers from Arizona who will probably accept the digital windfall for what it is — a bagatelle, a minor prank of nature, of little consequence.

In the late '20s, Sixto Rosie ran the *Palacio de las Putas* (Palace of the Whores) way the hell out in the country on the road to Rio Pescadero, long before

Texas and Nevada cashed in on their rural chicken ranches, and she offered a brand of entertainment of incalculable good fun, even to those who did not wish to sample the pastry.

She served *quesadillas* dripping with cheese, along with Gulliver-sized frog legs from the mammoth croakers in the river. Her drinks were never suspect, being concocted with *agua potable*, so there was no fear, at least, of contracting those Latin bioforms which more commonly attack the gringo viscera *north* of the *huevos* (literally, eggs). But her *piece de resistance* was a library of mild porno films-of-the-day which catapulted a skittery group of Daisy May milkmaids into flatchested celluloid fame in the backwater saloons of that era and which, today, with their ubiquitous goateed farmer hiding in the bushes as the ladies unclothe to take a dip in the back-40 swimmin' hole, still rank among the funnier episodes in the annals of way-off-Broadway humor.

Ars gratia artis.

No one ever took these films seriously, even, I understand, when they were first made, and the extent of the porn, being as constricted as it was and limited to voyeurism, lent the epics to wide distribution to Elk and Moose clubs and thousands of private thee-ayters from Moose Jaw to (obviously) Mexicali. Sixto Rosie's singular claim was that she had more of these films than anyone west of the Pecos and that one of the milkmaids, Alice McGarrett, had actually worked for a while at the *Palacio* while "at liberty" from the more profitable monkeyshines associated with the cinema arts.

I only met Sixto Rosie once, at a political shindig in Phoenix, and at 50 she was stunning. At a younger age she was even more ravishing, I am told by leering old timers, and there was not a man in the Baja Territories who would not put up a week's pay for a tumble in Rosie's satin-covered hay, but Rosie was, except for her very early days, untouchable, an olive-eyed, mantilla'd lady of charm and wit.

"It would not be fair to the girls," she told desperate suitors, "to be in competition with their employer." And so she remained the most thoroughly desirable woman as far west as Los Angeles, where it was said that world-practiced European coquettes plied the ancient trade, and as far north as San Francisco, where the Paris-educated granddaughters of the railroad and mining men were entertaining on the sly from their manses on Nob Hill.

The real reason for Rosie's abstinence was more true to form, I thought, than to spare her girls' feelings, and was told to me some years ago by a cattle buyer from Barstow who, he claimed, had Rosie's confidence for many years. He was long a chronicler of her adventures from his post at the old De Anza Hotel bar in Calexico.

Rosie, the cattleman said, had fallen in love with a young *vaquero* (cowboy) named James Beldon who worked the ranches over near Tucson and Bisbee and places like that and who only came around the *Palacio* once every three months and then only to see the dirty movies. Shy, he was, but powerful handsome, and there wouldn't be any other way he would marry Rosie but that she should go straight. Well, Rosie did go straight and Beldon married her, but about two months after the wedding he got in a card game over in Juarez and shot a man. For some reason, the law took him all the way back to Mexicali and put him in jail there. He would be there forever, the judge told Sixto Rosie, and she got her back up. She found the men who were responsible for keeping Beldon in jail or letting him out, sort of a parole board, and she got to every one of them systematically. Found out where they lived, where they drank, where their tender spots were. Most of them, of course, were family men and they were also big shots in Mexicali politics, so she just got to each one of 'em and "'ticed 'em" to bed. Afterward, she would pop her big question. A little favor. So Beldon got out in six months. Only thing is, he ran away with the postmistress from Wickenburg, Arizona. Seems they had been corresponding all the time he was in the jail.

"Well, Rosie didn't want anything to do with men after that, other than to take their money, and it's surprising she ever did that with good cheer, though she did."

Today, there is a big wall in the statehouse in Mexicali that is missing a pair of red woolen socks which should pridefully be there, a memento of Baja's history. And old Sixto Rosie is doing well in cantaloupes.

EL COYOTE AND THE
MAGIC MUSHROOMS

There used to be a famous sporting-goods store, headquartered in New York, called Abercrombie and Fitch. Now, I think, the name is used for a string of stores featuring fashion clothing. The old Abercrombie's was what my wife calls a "wish" store, i.e., the prices were so high that very few people went there to buy — they went to play Walter Mitty.

For years, each winter, I was puzzled by the uneven row of wet little spots on the store's steamed-up display window, until one day I realized that I, too, was pressing my nose against the glass to inspect a gold-lamé camping outfit designed specifically for traversing the polar ice cap.

Abercrombie's was a cruel hoax for would-be explorers who thought that by dressing the part and owning all the paraphernalia they would become instant Sherpa tribesmen.

The world is full of these pseudo-outdoorsmen. There are few real men to match the mountains.

One of the genuine articles is an overgrown troll named Dar Mikkelson. Like T. J., he too is legendary in Baja. Because he could catch a can of salmon in a damp sponge, the Mexicans call him "El Coyote." I know that designation sounds like Hollywood hype, but I'm stuck with it. It is a verity.

Now in his early fifties, Coyote is a rangy, diffident, Tom Selleck type, but with straw hair and a moon face that is sometimes the texture and color of Casey's Premium Brand Corned Beef. When Coyote dies, I predict that many of the marginal distillers of tequila will snuff out their fires. But the cactus juice has not yet fatally diminished his pace.

Coyote is what I call a "loper." That is, you think he is just dawdling on the trail and all of a sudden you find yourself alone. He is at the top of the mountain, 10 miles away. And he has dinner ready.

By my calculations, Coyote has probably caught more fish in Baja on rod and reel than any other man alive. I base this conclusion on the fact that since he was a young man he has averaged about 24 hours a week at sea, even allowing for long layoffs in the wintertime. And he never fails to come in with a load of fish. When he pops into his fragile aluminum boat, you can almost envision the sea bass jumping all the way to the horizon trying to get out of his way.

But you would never know to look at him that he is Baja's *numero uno* angler. He is not real Abercrombie. In fact, he wears a tattered Marine Corps field jacket, and his "tackle box" is one of the pockets.

Among his many other adventures: On his way back from the Yucatan as a youth, Coyote once tarried for a year with the Zapotec Indians in a small jungle village down near Salina Cruz — a place on tropical Tehuantepec Bay, called "La Ventosa." That was in the early '50s and La Ventosa is still not on the major road maps. As you can imagine, it was the kind of exotic destination Abercrombie-wishers wished for — wild pineapples and papayas, plump iguanas behind every fern, rich coffee toted by runners from the mountains in Chiapas, and a local entrepreneur who would wander in from the forest once a week with a shoulder pole bearing two casks of *mescal* (big bad booze) that would make your toenails curl up like those paper horns you blow at New Year's Eve parties.

Coyote hunted with an ancient flintlock that he had put into working condition after one of the tribe had unearthed it from the compost of the jungle floor. The Indians made their own sisal line and nets for *lisa* (mullet) and *robalo* (snook), and stroked in dugout canoes to a reef farther out in the bay for *pargo* (dog snapper), *pez gallo* (roosterfish), *huachinango* (red snapper), *toro* (Jack Crevalle), and beyond for an occasional *pez vela* (sailfish). Coyote went with them and showed them how to double their catch by using a screwball lure he had forged out of an old fork handle.

You must fix in your mind that a "very tall" Zapotec pushes maybe four feet, and Coyote is six-foot-four. In a canoe full of the Indians, he must

40

have looked like Kamehameha on an outrigger throne. Coyote claims that the *cacique* (chief) proffered some maidens to keep him warm at night, but he (Coyote) could never find them, since they were always scurrying about down there in the region of his belt buckle.

I don't believe Coyote's demurrer, for it is said that a race of giants, the hue of corned beef, now lopes silently through the jungle in that land. But, coincidentally, an errant Zapotec from Ventosa, whom I nudged while scrounging in a nearly spent Baja potato field last year, confirmed the rest of the story.

Strangely, the diminutive aborigine kept referring to Coyote as "Bwana." He was surprised to learn from my lips that Coyote had apparently been using an alias during the jungle hiatus.

Coyote has an independent sense of humor. As "Bwana," he held court under a palm-thatched *ramada* on the coconut beach and wailed old barroom ditties, which he translated into Zapotec for the amusement of the little fishermen. Toward evening, at the time of the *crepusculo* (sundown), he watched the flaming orb descend as he dozed off in his hand-wrought hammock to the scratchy music of the scuttle crabs and the last faint cries of the leaf-mottled *papagayos* (parrots).

Why did he leave? Lonely for his own kind, I suspect.

I can picture him there like E.T., swaying in mescaline solitude on the moon-shadowed *playa*, pointing at the distant stars and moaning "Coyote phone home."

Last week I was standing at stormy dawn on our Baja beach, watching Coyote deftly maneuver his thimble-skiff out through a calamitous surf, a couple of battered home-wrapped fishing rods and a pre-Columbian outboard motor belying his expertise.

Two Abercrombie-and-Fitch fellows, down from the States, decked out in the latest fishing toggery and clutching a fortune in mint-condition gear, sidled up to me and pointed at the lonely, disreputable figure in the tiny boat.

"You know," said one, "my friend here is a real pro. He's fished down here in Baja three or four times now, and he says that guy out there doesn't know what he's doing in that little boat. You know the guy? You think he'll be okay?"

I lit a Fiesta cigarette and took two long pulls on it.

"I don't know," I coughed. "It looks pretty rough out there."

The "pro" shook his head. "Yeah, the dumb jerk probably thinks he's a real outdoorsy type. I'll tell ya. Ya gotta know what you're doin' down here in Baja or it can be real dangerous. Amateurs like that guy out there are a dime a dozen."

"Yeah," said the pro's friend, "there's a million of 'em."

Although I pride myself in being a naturalist, a sportsman and a wilderness survivor, Coyote always

42

seems to know more about the details of these avocations than I do. I guess I am a little jealous of his expertise at living well without, apparently, doing any work whatsoever. Coyote has dwelt comfortably in Mexico for 25 years on the *interest* from $12.80 he once picked up in a poker game in Gardena.

He lives by hook or crook off the land, and Julia Childs can't touch him in the kitchen.

For a lifetime, the sea, the wilderness mountains, the deserts and the jungle have been his playgrounds. But I suspect he could bounce into a big-city phone booth and emerge with a game dinner for 12. He fashions an octopus salad that is extra-cosmic, his smoked yellowtail *sings*, and his rabbit stew would be billed as *lapin d'or* at Maxim's and go for 50 simoleons a plate.

Coyote is always the first to find the edible plants on the river bank. He gathers his sage, oregano, and anise from the hills. He seldom returns from his 10-mile "morning stroll" without an armful of wild celery, watercress, *tomatillos*, or other assorted free groceries with which God has mysteriously cluttered his path.

Wherever Coyote goes in Mexico, hunger ceases. He takes pleasure in sharing his bounty. He hung around my place last summer to help me build a boat, and one day I realized we hadn't been to the grocery store in two months.

But he has a terrific tendency to flaunt his superiority.

Coyote comes to me one day and says, "Can I put

43

some stuff in your freezer tomorrow? You can have half of it."

"Sure," says I, "what's the commodity?"

"Mushrooms," says Coyote.

"Mushrooms?" says I. "I haven't seen any mushrooms in the stores lately. And there sure as hell aren't any wild ones 'cause I'm looking for them all the time."

"Yeah," says Coyote, "but I know a secret place where there'll be wild ones tomorrow. All you want."

Then he goes over to my bar and mixes himself a drink in exchange for this coded information.

I amble outside like I'm going to water the tomatoes and I start kicking around in the dirt. I walk up the hill and inspect the cow flops and road apples where the first mushrooms usually appear. I go farther afield and peer under the sage and around the clumps of wild *marguerites* in the neighboring canyons. Coyote, I deduce, has just snookered me out of a half a liter of tequila while I am barging around the tundra. A wild mushroom chase.

I storm back to the casa and go the cupboard for the recipe book that came with the freezer. Nothing about mushrooms.

"You can't freeze mushrooms," I toss out, somewhat belligerently.

"Sure you can," Coyote says, disappointed in my stupidity. "You just parboil 'em for three or four minutes, dunk 'em in ice water and freeze 'em."

While Coyote is pouring himself another buzzer of tequila, I rifle through the kitchen cabinet for the

44

Joy of Cooking. I find (essentially) this: "Mushrooms — parboil for 3 ½ minutes, plunge in ice water five minutes, then freeze." The guy has outsmarted me again. I am now quivering with inadequacy.

"Well," I say, lashing out with a weak rejoinder, "there are no goddam mushrooms anyway. I just looked."

"Tomorrow," Coyote says mysteriously, pouring another dollop. "Three days of rain, two days of sunshine. Seventy-eight degrees. Secret place. The mushrooms will come up tomorrow."

Coyote outweighs me, or at this point I would belt him.

The following morning there is a clatter in the toolshed where I keep the freezer. I drag myself out of bed and there is Coyote carrying an empty five-gallon bucket.

"I cooked those mushrooms and put them in your freezer," he says. "I don't need 'em right now. I got another bucket in the pickup."

"Another *bucket*? How are you going to eat a whole bucket of mushrooms?" I wonder aloud.

"I'm not," he says. "Gonna trade 'em. Chata Fernandez has a new crop of beefsteak tomatoes and some pretty good corn. Want some?"

Half an hour later he is back with three dozen ears of corn, a sack full of vine-ripe tomatoes and a huge watermelon.

"She threw in the watermelon," he says, dumping the stuff on my kitchen table. "I'm going down the beach to get some octopus. The tide's just right. You

45

want some?"

"Yeah, if you get enough," I mutter. "Don't you want some of these vegetables?"

"Naw. I got two boxes full in the pickup."

"Coyote," I say, severely distressed. "What are you going to do with all those tomatoes?"

"Trade 'em. Tony Aguila just pulled in a trap full of good-sized crabs. You like crabmeat salad?"

"Love it," I say. "Love it."

"You got any bleach?" says Coyote.

"Bleach?"

"Yeah. For the octopus."

"You bleach the octopus?"

"Naw," he says, between pulls on the tequila. "You pour it in the hole in the rocks and the octopus comes out."

I give him the bleach.

Before he comes back with a huge sack of octopus, I go outside and notice that mushrooms, big as ping-pong balls, have popped up all over my front yard.

I can tell by the stubs that the grandest and most delectable have already been picked.

PAPPY O'TOOLE,
VAUDEVILLIAN

*Como telas de arañas son las
leyes, que prenden a las moscas
y no al milano.*
(The laws are like spider-
webs, catching the flies
and letting the hawk go
free.)
— old Baja *dicho*

When you can keep him awake, Pappy O'Toole is
a fascinating guy. He makes his coffee in a gym sock
and he's full of stories.

Pappy is the old-timer leprechaun I mentioned
early on in this tome who played the ukelele for
many years in vaudeville and who now peddles
high-test, private-label vodka with a rattlesnake in it.
Pap is so lovable, I hesitate to demean the canny old
charlatan, but in fairness to those of you who might
come to Baja looking for him, I must expose some of
his pranks for what they are, else thou shalt be
swindled. Pap does not have a mean bone in his
body, but if you look as though you might be carrying a little too much dinero for your own good, the
old scalawag can choose from any of several market-
tested redistribution-of-wealth programs at which

47

he is notoriously expert and he will happily more than rectify your indiscretion.

Pap is an artist at the shell game, three-card monte and a little stunt with matches called "pick up sticks," though it is more to his liking to use more sophisticated chicanery and he will go to any lengths to pull off a flim flam of monumental complexity. He especially loves a good sting operation and he tells me he has successfully carried one on for twelve years with a brace of ravenously greedy politicians who, up to this printing, think they are on the verge of enormous wealth which will be handed to them at any moment by "the crazy gringo who plays the *guitarrita* and would rather *siesta* than *fiesta*."

Pap does sleep a lot, there is no denying, but it is only, he says, to save himself from terminal boredom. Pap is 82.

Pap doesn't get a haircut often any more. Bleached straw shoots awry from beneath his Caterpillar Tractor cap, his eyes are yellowed and his face corrupted with hard times, desert sun and wind, alcohol, the pain of a faulty memory, long nights of turning in bed with agonizing arthritis and the constant fear that the plastic spaghetti where his arteries used to be will not do the job much longer. His smile, though, is frequent, if philosophical.

He doesn't shave often either, and his whole graybristle beard and moustaches are nicotine-stained to match his teeth. He is not careful about himself. "Not much sense," he says.

One short leg is bent inward 20 degrees at the

knee, so he waddles.

"Horse come down on me. Knocked the breath outa me. Didn't know nothin' fer three hours 'til I woke up. Shattered all them bones there, y'see, aroun' the knee. Down below, too. Put a splint on it. Pick handle it was. Didn't do no good though. Had to keep workin' and the damned thing kept slidin' loose. Horse was okay, though."

Pap talks in a coarse whisper.

"Nodes, y'know. Did two-a-day fer eighteen years, hollerin' them songs out to the boys in the back. The trick was, y'see, they had to name a song I didn't know. Well, plain and simple, they *wasn't* any songs I didn't know, only I had to yell out the words and do some fancy strummin'. Well it finally jes' blew the vocal cords all to hell. That and the fags. Booze, too, I guess. Hell, ain't nothin' I like's good for me."

Pap's arthritis and nodes got too bad to play professionally any more, so after his last performance at the Valencia Theater on Genesee Street in Waukegan, Illinois, in the spring of 1934 he put his trunks on the 20th Century Limited and headed for Los Angeles, then for Arizona, "to get the cure or die."

"Oh, it was bad, y'know. Walked aroun' like a dead man. Couldn't sleep nothin' at all. Desert wasn't warmed up yet from the winter, neither. Thought it wasn't doin' me no good 'tall. Put a board over one of them holes over back of town. Lotta holes over on that hill. Deep they was, but filled with water sixty feet down. Couldn't mine 'em no more,

49

couldn't get 'em pumped out. Tombstone it was. Tombstone, Arizona. Hell of a place to die. Jes' lay there every night on that board an' prayed I'd go to sleep an' roll over an' fall down that deep hole. Never woulda known what hit me. Woulda hit my head on the way down, fer sure. Never did fall off the board, though. Pretty soon it warmed up and the artha-ritis jes' went away."

"What did you do then, Pap?"

"Well, all they was doin' in that town was talkin' 'bout diggin'. Gold fever, y'know, though the diggin' was pretty well over by then. Anyway, after a while I got to know what to look for an' how to get it out of the ground. Feller lost his leg with the diabetes an' sold me all his stuff. Picks an' shovels an' pans an' a hunnerd things I didn't need. Old burra, too. Alice, she was. Gentle as a kitten and strong as an ox. Sweet baby, she was. Me an' she walked all the way through that Sonora desert and clear up into the Mojave.

"Finally wound up on top of the Old Dad Mountains, up there near Kelso, toward the Nevada line. Kelso, Amboy, Baghdad, I knew all them towns. Wasn't much then, ain't much now. Started diggin' me a hole up there on top of the Old Dads. Used chisels an' fertilizer dynamite. Lucky I didn't blow m'own head off. Pretty country it was, though. Up high, y'see. Bighorns useter come 'roun every mornin' to drink outa my trough. Five years I spent in that tunnel. Nickel and silver, it was. No gold. Ore wasn't too good neither. Got in two hunnerd feet an' give up. In the end, all the mice had turned into blind albinos. Pink eyes, they had. No light, y'see. I slept in there durin' the winter. Pack rats useter steal my fags. Money, too. Couldn't leave a quarter layin' round. But that desert sure was good for the artharitis."

"What did you do then, Pap?"

"Well, the wild jack burras ran off with Alice, so I went down there to Ludlow an' dug 'nother hole. Near the old Chase copper mine, it was. Got me some nice peacock ore and some pretty good gold. Lotsa leetle nuggets in it. Just a pocket, though. Took it all out an' buried it, 'fore anybody knew what I was doin'. Still got a hole full of it up there. Lot of it down here, too, buried there on that hillside."

He nodded toward the mountain in the distance.

"Say, you want a drink?" he croaked.

"God, that's ugly," I shuddered when I saw the rattlesnake in the vodka. As he tipped the Sparkletts bottle, which was mounted in a gimbaled wrought-iron stand, the rattler (a two-footer) writhed in the clear liquid as though alive. The mouth was propped wide open with a wad of cotton, so the fangs were sticking out.

"Well, the snake surely is ugly," Pap grinned, looking up from the jug he was filling, "but that's my sizzle, sonny. Ain't sellin' the steak, sellin' the sizzle. Hell, you can buy *vodka* anywhere. 'Sides, the price is right. This one's on the house." After that we were friends.

Pap called me "Harriet."

Perhaps I should explain that.

It was at that first meeting over Pap's vodka jug that he looked at me strangely when I told him my name.

"Hoctor?" he said, with narrowed eyes. Then he correctly spelled it out. "Ain't a relation to Harriet Hoctor, are you?"

"Yes," I said. "She's my father's sister. My aunt."

"Be damned! You don't say," Pap said, shaking my hand with enthusiasm.

"Why I was on a bill with her at the Palace. 1927, I think. Yep. With Ethel Merman. Harriet Hoctor. Toe dancer, she was. Great act. Pretty as a picture. In the Follies later. Old Ziggy had an eye for her, I think. But she always had a little kid with her. Wouldn't tell nobody who the daddy was. Cute little feller. Big hit backstage. Fanny (Brice) useter get dressed up fer doin' "Baby Snooks" an' the two of 'em would walk aroun' back there so's you couldn't tell which one was the kid. Nobody never made a pass at Harriet 'causa that kid."

"That was me," I said.

"Who was you?" Pap said.

"The little kid. I lived with Aunt Harriet for sixth months in the Algonquin Hotel. Guess I served a purpose," I said, reflecting happily on my career as a childhood beard.

"Well, thunder!" Pap exploded. "Lookatcha how ya growed!"

From that day on, Pap called me "Harriet." "It's easier," he said. "Easy ta remember. Why? Ya ain't got no feelin's 'bout it, do ya? Ya don't have none a them *tendencies*?" Then he cackled and jumped around in the dust until he had to collapse on a nail keg.

Now. The sting.

"Harriet," Pap whispered from his nail keg one day, looking up from his favorite Martin uke with the mother-of-pearl inlay, "that song I just played is from *Hitchy-Koo*. Grace La Rue sang it and Al von Tilzer wrote it. Big hit. Made her famous. Now I'll tell you what's called. It's called *I May Be Gone For A Long, Long Time*. Puts me in mind to maybe take a trip. Been thinkin' of goin' down to the mine."

"What mine, Pap?" I said in my best straight-man tone.

"Well, Harriet, I got a little glory hole goin', y'see. Nothin' much, but she keeps me goin'. She's down near the old deLacey diggin's at Punta Final. I thought mebbe you 'n Coyote'd like to come down there and catch us some grub. She's smack up agin' the Gulf, y'see, an' I kin oogle the fish jumpin' from where I set. There's fish ta glore."

"Galore," I corrected.

"That's what I said, ta glore."

"My God, Pap, you mean you've been mining down there? That's illegal as hell for a gringo. If they catch you they'll throw the key away."

"Not likely. Got me a few real important boys tied into the deal."

"Mexicans?"

"Hee hee. Honchos. Politicians. Real big."

"You mean it's all legal?"

The smoke from his Mexican cigarette was making his eyes water and without touching it he spat it out of his mouth into the dust.

"Well, acourse, there ain't no paper work, y'see, but those are pretty important fellers." He cackled again.

"Good grief, Pap, you're crazy," I said. "What are you taking out of there, gold?"

He exhaled the smoke from a newly lit Fiesta and laughed.

"Salt," he said. "Got me a salt mine." Then he waved his hand in the air, dismissing the subject.

Two hours later the three of us jammed into Pap's old Land Rover along with Coyote's case of tequila, six cases of beer, assorted fishing gear, sleeping bags, a big iron skillet and two bottles of cooking oil. Pap's fat calico cat, Pismo, sat on top of the seat-back behind me and licked my hair.

A mysterious wooden crate filled most of the back of the Land Rover.

"What's in the box?" Coyote grunted, craning around to inspect the cargo.

"You'll see," Pap wheezed, staring straight ahead, and lurched out of the yard, between the oleanders, sending Pismo into a near-perfect back flip to the top of the crate, where she stayed for the rest of the trip.

We threaded our way through the lush vineyards of Santa Tomas, then navigated the switchbacks along a hundred miles of coastal mountains to the farm town of San Quintín on the coastal plain, bivouacking for the night behind Pavarotti's cantina. Pavarotti was out of ammunition so he could not shoot holes in the ceiling and he was too drunk to sing, but Pap and the bassett hound did *Oh What A Pal Was Mary* to the strains of the uke, with the dog turning in a creditable performance despite the fact that the tune had been written half a century before it (the dog) was whelped and the melody was riddled with sticky transitions. Even Pap applauded, which is to say that the turn would probably have been a smash on the Orpheum Circuit.

At dawn, Coyote woke us with a breakfast of Oro coffee and some kind of delicious eggs (small, with yolks of deep orange) followed by tin bowls of sweet *tunas* (cactus pears) and goat's milk, all of mysterious origin. Then we drove through a dust storm at El Rosario and up into the hot and thin-aired *boojum* forest of the high Vizcaino desert.

To call it a forest is perhaps misleading, because the "trees" are not trees at all, but plants — giant cirios, or *boojums*, spindly and thorn-bristled, vying for space with pitajayas; house-high cardons with supplicating arms and riddled with elf-owl holes; ocotillos; fuzzy *chollas*; and dozens of other unworldly cacti and ankle-low plants with desperate leaves and minute wildflowers, all of which make this the most interesting desert in the world to the botanist. In the sharp sun of early morning, the decomposed granite of the desert floor sparkled. Quail were everywhere.

Boulders here are often house-sized, evenly cloven with wind-rounded edges, sometimes piled one upon the other. The desert is a Dali plain, yet exhilarating and without sorrow. Overriding all is the *boojum*, the Marcel Marceau of this unique region, sometimes rising ramrod straight, other times mocking those among us with twisted souls.

Some times of the year the Vizcaino turns into a furnace and the devil pumps the bellows. Most plants cannot survive here, yet *boojums* love it and sometimes grow to sixty feet.

Their chief characteristic is that no two have exactly the same configuration. Some shoot heavenward as if by plan. Others twist and turn in their growth, maturing to shapes which defy imagination.

No real value has been found for these trees when alive.

They are just fun to look at.

When dead, their sunbleached husks are prized and used as ornamental ranch fences, lamp bases, planters and architectural facing.

Those who do not wonder at the *boojum* forest, those who cannot abide the stillness, are such sad people. I once drove through the forest with a noisy young engineering student who read *Mad Magazine* all the way and laughed hollowly as he quoted long passages against my will.

Now, in a better time, Pap and Coyote remained silent.

We turned off the highway below Josephina's *rancho* at Santa Inez, meandered across ten miles of the humpy Chapala perimeter and into the canyon of Calamajue, crisscrossing its meager stream, shouldered by jadite cliffs and outcroppings of pink and white and lavender, tufa and crystal, once agonized, now at rest.

A lynx ran before us while the hidden creatures slept.

We took our time.

In the late afternoon we rose to the last desert crest and the Gulf lay before us, at the foot of the broad alluvial plain — the Gulf, that spectacular turquoise Aegean, studded by the volcanic *Islas Encantadas* (Enchanted Islands), home of a million sea birds, on pumice pinnacles of fishy realms.

It is hard to describe the feeling upon first seeing the Sea of Cortez.

"The very air here is miraculous and the outlines of reality change with the moment," Steinbeck wrote in the log.* "That sea of mirages and timelessness is a very magical place... the sky sucks up the land and disgorges it... a dream hangs over the whole region, a brooding kind of hallucination."

"All night the hissing rush and splash of hunters and hunted went on in waters almost solid with fish, swarming, hungry, frantic fish, incredible in their voraciousness."

"John ranked that book with *East of Eden*," my friend Ray Cannon once told me. "But he was always

* John Steinbeck, *The Log From the Sea of Cortez,* Viking Press.

sorry he couldn't quite do the Sea justice."

From the sublime to the ridiculous: Pappy revealed a flaccid penis and wrote his name in the glittery sand in front of the mine.

"Heathcliff, I call it," Pap laughed, giving the member a final shake. "Witherin' Heights. Hee, hee."

Coyote crossed the T in O'Toole.

Despite Coyote's great strength, it took all he had to pull the mystery crate to the tailgate of the Land Rover.

It was full of rocks.

"Some pretty good stuff," Pappy said, chipping at a piece with a hand pick. "It's the stuff I brought down from Ludlow. Got a leetle nugget in this one, y'see?" Then he filled a canvas sack and walked back twenty feet into the hole to sprinkle his "salt."

After half a dozen trips he came out brushing his hands and spanking the front of his khakis.

"That oughter hold 'em fer another year," he said, pulling the empty crate to the ground and setting the camp stove atop it.

Coyote, apparently in on the joke, laughed and loped away down a rocky path to the water's edge, bearing a jug of tequila and a long surf rod.

"Well?" I said.

"Well what?"

"You going to tell me the story?"

"What story? Oh, y'mean the ore?"

"Yeah, the ore."

"Well, y'see, Harriet, it all has to do with pricin'

58

structure, an' it's terrible complicated, so I think I better wait'll t'nite when we got some time. Gotta make camp right now. Be dark soon."

"Pricing structure?"

"Pricin' structure."

That night around the campfire, coyotes yipping close and a fearless desert mouse eating bits of barbecued yellowtail fillet out of his cupped hand (Pismo was off somewhere on safari), Pappy told me this:

"Well, y'see it's all a matter of greed and the price a man's willin' to pay.

"It all started with a fella named Montoya, useter ride with the man they call 'La Law' up there in the high Sierra, the San Pedro Martir country in back of the Svensen Ranch. Now Montoya was just as crooked as La Law was straight. The two of 'em was lawmen of some kind — trackers, dog shooters when the rabies come up, fire spotters, game wardens, sheriffs, all rolled up into one I guess, 'ceptin Montoya always had his hand out fer the *mordida*. The bite, y'know.

"Well a while back, La Law was busy takin' some ranch guests mule packin' up into the snow country and Montoya come down here to get his feet warm. Caught me diggin' a hole down the line from here toward Calamajue. Down by the fish camp. Had the goods on me all right. I had a pickup fulla onyx and a couple nuggets on me big as strawberries."

He tugged on a thong hanging around his neck and a $200 chunk of raw gold appeared from beneath the V in his shirt.

"Like this'n here," he said.

"Well, Montoya could see I wasn't runnin' no half-baked rock-hound operation but was a fer-sure prospector, makin' a leetle money out of it. Dang little if he was to know the truth of it.

"But he wasn't gonna turn me in, nosiree, just wanted his cut. I told the feller I didn't have nothin' in that hole he was lookin' at, but that I had some new diggin's up in back of the ridge there where I thought there might be some pretty good stuff. Looked real promisin', I said. Took this here strawberry nugget out to show him."

The old man tucked the nugget back in his shirt and gazed down at the mouse, which had apparently gone to sleep in his hand.

"Cute little feller, ain't he?" he said.

"Well, this feller Montoya, his eyes got so big they'd a liked to pop. Ain't nothin' in the world more excitin' to a man than the sighta gold 'fore it's been turned into pocket money. One little piece like this" — Pap patted his shirt — "they see whole mountains of it. 'Course he wanted to know right away where it was, how much there was in the hole. Woulda cut my throat right there if he knew where the hole was. Told him I didn't know yet how much gold there was. Told him he had to wait. Then I took my lucky piece out of the collectin' sack. Piece a ore big as my fist. Had a leetle tiny piece a gold in it, looked like a bird, with its wings out like this. Oh that got him excited all right. Liked to pee his pants. Only worth a

60

few dollars, maybe, but you'd a thunk I hit the jackpot. Y'see, seein' gold right there in the rock, sittin there just fer the takin', why that does somp'n to a man. He looks aroun' and he sees these rocks all around him, and he figgers every one of 'em's got a bird in it, hee, hee, or a bigger critter. So I give him the rock and tell him to come back and away he goes. Month later we met down there at the fish camp an' I give him a little boxa this Ludlow ore. Told him I'd struck it rich.

"Acourse, he went right away and had it assayed. Feller in town told him it was purty good stuff but it wasn't from around here. Wrong matrix. No rocks like these in Baja. Well acourse, if it had been you or me, we woulda smelled a rat right away.

"But not old Montoya. Too greedy. He figgered I'd hit somp'n new that the engineers just didn't know about. All the better for him, he figgered. Oh, he had the whole seven cities of Cibola in his back pocket, he did. Aztec gold, fer sure."

"Why didn't he just mine it himself?" I said.

"Well, he didn't know nuthin' about it, y'see. Didn't know a handpick from a hoe. 'Sides, I wouldn't tell him where the hole was. Why, hell, he woulda shot me an' hired somebody to do the diggin'. S'long as I kep' givin' him leetle chunksa that ore, he figgered he'd hold off. Y'see, I told him we didn't want to let nobody know where that hole was, 'cause first thing y'know it'd be gov'ment proppity. Best thing, I told him, was to get all the good stuff out quiet like, an' bury it in the sand sommers else.

Told him it'd take maybe two-three years. Well, that got him all excited too. 'Y'mean there's that much?' he said. 'Why sure,' I said. 'Could be more. But we tip our hand right now, we're gonna wind up with none of it. Can't take it to a refinery little by little or somebody's gonna know where the hole is. Best thing to do is take it an' hide it, then get it across the border n'draw our paychecks.'"

"What about the politicians?" I said.

"What politicians?"

"You said you had an okay from a couple of politicians."

"Hee hee. Yeah. Well y'see, old Montoya had to ring them in 'cause he needed some money."

"What for?"

"Why, to pay me fer my diggin'. An' to keep my mouth shut, acourse. They figgered they'd all broke the bank."

"Yes," I said, "but twelve years you've been doing this? With no payoff? What the hell is keeping them on the hook?"

"Well they're greedy, y'see. An' the price is right."

"What do you mean?"

"Well, every year I give 'em a few more rocks. Tell 'em I found a whole new vein. Tell 'em we've gotten up close to maybe a million dollars or more. Oughta see their eyes light up at that. Kids in a candy store, they are. So they give me another ten thousand pesos an' wait."

(10,000 pesos was about $800 at the time.)

"With no payoff?" I said.

62

"Oh, they're gettin' a payoff. They're gettin' hope, y'see. The very foundation of greed. An' it's cheap enough so they ain't gonna get *real* pushy. Why ten thousand pesos, that's nothin' ta them politicians. Not when they're lookin' at a ten-million-peso-or-more return. If I was ta hold 'em up fer more than that, acourse, mebbe they'd want ta get right down to brass tacks. If I asked for less, why they'd think I had a dry hole. The price is right, y'see. It's all a matter of pricin' structure. They don't know where the hole is, but they don't want to let go of that dream. S'long as I show 'em some new ore once in a while, why they got hope."

"Don't they spy on you?" I said.

"Oh, they folly me all the time. Montoya comes down here with his pickup and that appaloosa horse he rides. Peeks around from behind the rocks, he does. But I come and I go. He can't watch me all the time. 'Sides, ain't no hole anyway, ceptin' this phony one here. I only dug this one to make things good and confusin'. He knows this ain't the right hole, but he cain't figger why I dug it or why I salt it. Ain't no *real* glory hole, acourse."

"My God," I said, "you mean you're collecting *mordida* from two Mexican politicians?"

"Three," he said. "An' a sheriff. Don't fergit Montoya. He puts up parta the pot."

"Three? I thought there were only two politicians in on the deal."

"Well, they was. But those two started gettin' antsy fer *some* kind of a payoff, so last week I went over

63

to Mexicali and cut their boss in. Now he's all excited he's gonna get rich, too. Thinkin' about cuttin' the other boys out. Told 'em he'd throw 'em all in the slammer if anything happened to me. Guess this new feller'll be good for another 10 years. By that time I'll be dead."

"Pappy, you're amazing," I said, genuinely impressed.

"No, Harriet," he said. "Mankind's amazin'. Dumb as he is, goin' to the moon to pick up a buncha worthless rocks."

Before Pappy could move, Pismo came flying out of the darkness fast as a shadow and snatched the mouse out of Pap's hand. Took the creature down in one gulp.

"That'll teach you to get cocky," Pap said sadly to his empty hand, and he drifted off to sleep with his arms crossed gently over the inlaid uke.

Is Pap's story true?

My God, who knows?

With Pap one never guesses which shell the pea is under.

However, there is no denying the importance of pricing structure.

And the intensity of Man's greed, of course.

MY MOTHER THE DOCTOR

Try to get a clear picture of Campo Loco* in your mind, because many of the tales I will tell are centered here or in its environs. It is the small Mexican/American community where Sylvia and I have now lived for many years.

The camp is far north of the boojum forest, in cooler climes, at the edge of the Pacific. It is about 100 miles south of the border from San Diego. There are two fishing shacks and 28 houses, from ramshackle to pretentious, the latter built back from the beach. It is not a tract. There are dusty roads between the homes, and flowers of every description.

The view from the camp is extraordinary. One looks across Bahia de Todos Santos, the Bay of All Saints, toward the port and tourist town of Ensenada, 10 miles distant.

On sharp, clear days, which are frequent, one can see 50 miles of dazzling, continuous coastline.

---

* In Baja, until a community gets a telephone, a cop and a politician, it is called a "camp."

Ten miles seaward, the Todos Santos Islands guard the entrance to the bay. They are shot through with sea caves, and it is rumored locally that the sight inspired Robert Louis Stevenson to write *Treasure Island*. (His mother lived, for a time, in Ensenada.)

20 miles to the east are the foothills of Juarez, the Sierra, the often-snowcapped backbone of Baja.

The climate is moderate, with prevailing afternoon north-westerlies. Days are usually brilliant, in the 70s nearly all year. Summers are glorious. Hot but dry. Lazy and slow. Summer days are long, nights languid. As the camp is well out of the smog lanes and miles from city lights, the night sky is rampant with stars.

We especially love the casa where we live, at the outskirts of the camp.

The casa sits about 30 yards from the edge of a 100-foot sea cliff which drops down to a small, private beach. An adjacent dirt road winds downward through a canyon to a storm-wracked jetty and a small boat ramp clogged with lobster skiffs, or "pangas," as the Mexicans call them.

A few hundred yards offshore is a half-mile-long kelp bed where sea lions play and where, in winter, barnacled, 30-foot gray whales can be observed frolicking with their calves. The kelp bed is a favorite spot for divers and fishermen from all over the world because it is teeming with scrappy bull bass and, sometimes, toothy "log" barracuda, flashy bonito and the king of the inshore gamefish, the rainbow-hued yellowtail. The bay is known as "the yellowtail capital of the world."

Behind the casa are whalebacked mountains covered with chaparral—cactus, sage, wild oregano and, in the spring, white and yellow daisies, orange poppies and blue lupine. These mountains terminate in a fiercely rugged point that juts into the sea to the west. There are foxes, deer, possums, owls, giant ospreys and things that go bump in the night in those hills. Our front yard is home for coveys of quail, a pair of roadrunners and a resident lynx which ambles by every morning in search of ground squirrels. Our daily walk is an adventure.

In the fall, we usually catch the tail ends of two or three "chubascos," moist, tropical storms from the southern seas.

And for a couple of months in the winter, all hell breaks loose. Three- and four-day storms bring cold, torrential rains, nighttime temperatures plummet, roads are obliterated, houses are flooded. Electricity goes out for weeks at a time. The oil lamps come out.

These are the times we like best to come to the casa, though. There is a good library and a large Franklin fireplace at the end of our deep-carpeted living room. There are big clumps of rock-hard manzanita root that burn long and hot. There are fine fish mounts by Lyons and O'Haver and pictures of our old friends on the wall — Pappy O'Toole playing the ukelele in front of his vodka-still after the Federales left; the Reverend T.J. letting his prisoner out of the ice house; Mamacita doing a fandango with El Coyote, soaking wet. There are also reminders of expeditions long past, Sylvia's and mine, into the wilderness areas of Baja. A giant turtle shell. An old carving of an owl by our Indian friend who lives under the boulder in Calamajue Canyon. And, of course, the big portrait of Mamacita.

My adopted Mexican mother, Mamacita Rosita, lives just up the hill from me at Campo Loco. We have known each other for many, many years. She is my strongest link to the Mexican culture and I have more affection for her than I can say.

Mama is a wonderful old Baja pioneer, a landmark, really, who has only three expressions — a crinkly smile involving her whole face (which means things are OK); a desolate look of utter despair (the famous "Sad Indian" look), which means that things are not so good; and a grandmotherly pride face which she puts on when her great grandchildren are around. If someone had asked Norman Rockwell to do a painting of a very old Mexican woman with immense character and a lot of pain and suffering in her eyes, high Aztec cheekbones with leathery skin and character lines and all that, he would have come up with Mamacita on a not-so-good day.

Mama has wild wisps of silver hair which she constantly brushes back from her forehead with the back of her hand as she talks. Despite the fact that she speaks no English whatsoever, she has many, many gringo friends who speak no Spanish. I mean *friends*, not acquaintances. These relationships are maintained through a lot of sign language, Mama's enormously expressive face and *mucho* hugging.

Mamacita was a hellion when I first met her several decades ago. She made today's feminists look like Campfire Girls. She drank her Tecate beer from *caguamas* (the big bottles), and one could hear her clear up into the mountain arroyos when she had an argument. She could dance all night when she was 70. Now she is well into her eighties and has slowed down considerably. She has shrunk to about 80 pounds and hobbles around with a cane. In the past few years I have never seen her without the man-sized, fur-lined arctic combat boots which Roberto, the Music Man, gave her when she told him that her feet were always cold.

Every winter Mama prepares herself for her imminent death, and her hundreds of friends start adjusting themselves to that probability. But when the wild daisies start blooming in the spring, so does Mama, and shortly after the past winter she once again greeted me with the things-are-OK face and a self-imposed slap on her rump.

Mamacita doctored wounded soldiers during the Revolution and has taken care of most of my ailments for the past quarter century. She has a drug store in her backyard. She has herbs for diseases not invented yet, and somewhere in her garden there is an herb, I am sure, which will one day prevent a world plague.

Mama can diagnose and have the cure ready for any physical problem and many mental ones in just minutes. She prepares a variety of teas (made from herbs, roots and flowers) for various stomach complaints, fatigue, nervousness, languor, itch, ague and tennis elbow. In addition, she prescribes things like wearing red underwear for arthritis pain and putting match-head poultices on scorpion bites. If one has anxiety, one chews anise.

Everything Mama prescribes works instantly and with stunning effect.

I made the mistake recently of going to a neurologist in that citadel of modern medicine, La Jolla, California, and complaining very specifically of migraine headaches. I paid the man $110. He told me I had migraine headaches.

The headaches did not go away until I drank one of Mama's special teas made of nine flowers from a deep purple bougainvillea.

"Nine only," Mama said professionally. "No more, no less. And only the purple flower works."

Despite a spate of newfangled doctors being spewed out by the University at Guadalajara, medicine in Baja has reached what must surely be a Golden Age. All the knowledge of the Toltecs, Aztecs and mushroom-gobbling Olmecs has come together in a few bona fide wizards like Mama who would rather be caught with their red underwear showing than messing around with aspirin and stethoscopes and all that jazz.

Of course, Mama herself admits that she is only an amateur in the doctor game. The real wizzes are the *curanderas*, Mexico's answer to witch doctors or

70

shamans. These practitioners of the healing arts are officially outlawed by the government, yet maintain thriving illicit practices, and there are usually longer lines in their waiting rooms than there are at the offices of accredited medics.

Many of Baja's country women, especially, would never think of going to a government-approved stethoscope bearer to be pushed and prodded. They distrust the formality and the elegant airs of the graduate M.D. It is much more reassuring to have another comforting woman like themselves (but with special powers) press an amulet on them and lay her motherly, mystical hands on the oppressive aches and pains while chanting an ancient *nahuatl* cure poem.

Curanderas are not cheap. Many top-rated *curanderas* charge more than the university graduates, though I understand a few will accept trade items like chickens, goats, furniture or jewelry.

Mama works free.

Of course, the very best medicine in Baja, as elsewhere, is preventive medicine.

The best example of this is the care with which Mama picks the stones out of the frijoles before she cooks them.

Many marinades and sauces have been invented in Mexico to cover a variety of sins, and Mama knows them all. It is very difficult, for example, for a virulent bug to live long in her *carne asada* marinade, and when the *carne* (meat) is subsequently cooked to a frazzle, the jig is up for sure.

And Mama's *mole* sauce — the recipe is said to have been bestowed on the people by the feathered serpent god Quetzalcoatl in the 1300s — seems to disguise and purify the most iffy chicken. (Imagine covering a drumstick with cocoa and chile powder and you should get the picture.) It is most fortunate that Quetzalcoatl was unaware of the salubrious effects of aerosol bug sprays or we would all be sitting down today to Mexican combination plates drenched in malathion.

A few special words should be said for the chile pepper and the lemon. Mama is very big on these, and I think I know why.

I am not a medical man, but I simply cannot imagine a malicious microorganism surviving an attack by a Sacramento chile or one of those little green jobs that Mama uses for making colonic paint remover. And what a *chile poblano* does in cauterizing a gloopy alimentary canal is probably a thing of beauty to a trained gastroenterologist.

And, ahh, the lemon. The noble lemon.

A friend of mine maintains that if there were an embargo on all 1953 Chevrolet parts, Baja would come to a halt. I think a bad lemon crop would probably do the same thing. The lemon is as Baja as beans.

And lo and behold.

No scurvy.

Okay. So now the big question.

"What does one do when one has a Mexican hangover?" (The condition is known in Baja, rather aptly I think, as feeling "*crudo*," or "raw.")

Is there a cure?

Well, first, nobody ever got a hangover from *not* drinking tequila. Humorist Roger Price once described the antidote for "copelessness" (the inability to cope) as "avoidism." I suggest you heed his advice.

Knowing, however, that if you visit Baja you probably will not, I will give you the benefit of my considerable experience in the Mexican hangover department.

Menudo does not work.

Surefire remedies prescribed by your friends do not work.

Chopping wood does not work.

A dip in the ocean sometimes helps.

A hair of the chihuahua only prolongs the agony (presuming you can find a hair on a chihuahua).

Raw eggs make you retch. No more. No less.

You might try nine-flower tea from the bougainvillea. Purple only.

If it works, send Mamacita a check for $110.

Mamacita not only makes medicine, she also makes the most distinctive tortillas in the Americas. This is due, I am sure, to the quality of the bacteria on her paws. She always warms up for tortilla-making by running her hand through the coal-black hair of a variety of children who are eternally underfoot in her little casa.

I can always tell one of Mamacita's tortillas. It is absolutely ripe with flavor.

God knows, she has had enough practice making

tortillas. During the Revolution she worked in a little field commissary for the soldiers at a train embarkation point down in Sinaloa.

Her eyes light up when she talks about the *revolución*. Ahhh, those were the days. Shooting and drawn sabres. Trains full of hungry refugees and soldiers. Merriment and lovemaking in the camps.

And a cause.

As a revolution it was *pura Mexicana*, emotional as hell and altogether helter-skelter, with cut communications lines leaving gaggles of troops wandering around wondering where their next meal was coming from. Mama took care of that part of the revolution.

There is no use trying to copy Mamacita's tortillas. You simply don't have the props. First, there is the matter of the kids and the tousled hair. But even more important is *the* apron. Mama never starts any serious cooking without *the* apron and a *caguama* of Tecate beer. The apron is for wiping one's hands before touching the holy ingredients of the tortillas. With one good swipe, her hands take on the flavor of countless chiles, *tomatillos* and garlic cloves, plus *cilantro*, re-cycled lard and sufficient *bacteria exotica* to make a proper start at the cooking.

The *caguama* of Tecate is for divine guidance.

You should also know that Mama's tortillas can be made only with real Mexican flour. I once brought Mama a 50-pound sack of Pillsbury from the States and she immediately stuffed it under her bed, where I am sure it remains.

"*Muchas gracias*," she smiled, giving the sack a final love tap with her army boot. "If it does not make the weevils ill, I will surely use it."

Mama's humor devastates me.

She also has a great philosophy: You are born. You live as long as you can. You die.

That's it.

Every time I try to tell her there is more to life than that, or I start getting carried away with my own importance in the general scheme of things, she punctures my pretentious balloon with aplomb and leaves me searching anew for a *raison d'être*.

For example:

I was sitting around the rancho one day, working up to a siesta, when thoughts of pizza stirred me from my lethargy. Since the nearest pizza shop was across the border, 100 miles away, I determined to improvise. It was simple and quick. All I did was smear one of Mama's tortillas with olive oil, slap another tortilla on top, and smuck on some more olive oil. Then I started building the pizza on the homemade crust — pizza sauce, cheese, peppers, and my other favorite garbage. It was the best pizza I have ever eaten.

I made one of them for Mamacita.

"What do you call it?" she asked, sucking a long string of cheese into her mouth.

"Pizza," I answered with great pride. "It's an Italian dish."

She licked her lips, and stared off into space. Suddenly a look of infinite wisdom swept across

75

that beautiful face.

There was a hint of remembrance around her eyes, a flash of sudden joy at recalling long-forgotten memories.

"Where did you learn this thing?" she asked.

My head was swelling rapidly.

"Well, the top part is the way they make it in Italy, but the bottom part, the crust, is my own invention. I made it from two tortillas."

Mama smiled enigmatically.

"Don't you like it?" I asked.

"Oh yes. It is *muy sabrosa*," she shot back, straight-faced. "Delicious. It is what the Humi Indians used to make when I was a little girl in Culiacan."

I immediately stormed back to my casa and stared listlessly at the remaining tomato pie for two hours before lapsing into a solo game of "Find the Pope in the Pizza." Since I am an advanced player, I was not only able to identify seven papal profiles, clearly delineated among the bell peppers and anchovies, but I could actually name six of them, including two Innocents, a Benedict and the infrequently noted Boniface III from the early seventh century.

THE LAST LAUGH

At every funeral I have ever been to I have spotted someone in the crowd who smiles. Upon interrogation, I always find that the smiler is the very person who probably loved the deceased most.

Henry Kennedy's funeral was no exception.

Henry Kennedy was one of Mamacita's closest friends, and a friend of mine as well.

I like to think of him as Baja's Robinson Crusoe.

There were many British ships plying the waters around Punta Banda at the turn of the century. It was from one of these, he said (though I could never tell when he was kidding) that he jumped.

He adopted the Spanish version of his name, Enrique, and settled alone in a small cove at the northern end of Bahia Soledad.

The cove is a picture-perfect pirate's lair, and over the centuries more than one freebooter probably moored near its still waters. My friend Miguel Lopez Lopez recently found an ancient, barnacle-encrusted anchor while diving near the cove for sea urchins. It now proudly adorns our rock garden.

The cove itself — it is now known as "Kennedy's Cove" — is small, not more than a couple of hundred feet at its widest, reaching no more than a hundred yards into the side of the mountain hideaway Kennedy loved so much. It is almost impossible to find from seaward, virtually inaccessible by land and is perfectly protected from prevailing northwesterly seas. Its usually glassy waters are punctuated by craggy rock spires, atop the highest of which (a spindly pinnacle not more than six feet across at its top) is the ubiquitous wooden cross and now, if I am not mistaken, Kennedy's grave, hewn into the country rock.

When Kennedy first got there, the bottom of the cove and the adjacent sea caves were crawling with huge bull lobsters, some 10 pounds and more, and the submarine ledges were plastered with abalone (pinks, reds, blacks, and yellows, he said).

There were enormous sea scallops, too, and *chorros*, the big mussels Kennedy loved to roast over glowing manzanita.

Much later, SCUBA diving clubs from the United States changed all that, but Kennedy made a living selling off small portions of the largesse when he could.

He threw together a small wooden fishing shack about 30 feet from the pebbly beach, up on a narrow ledge. This became his hermitage for the better part of his life. From somewhere he dredged up an old rocking chair. Boaters passing by could scarcely believe their eyes when they spotted the solitary old man on the face of the cliff, in the middle of nowhere, rocking serenely in the sunset.

He was a shaggy old man who looked startlingly like W.C. Fields. For some reason he called me "Lad," and Lad it was as long as I knew him. He spoke of the moon and the tides, and it is said he had gold in the sea caves.

Kennedy was not always a loner.

Over the years, on his sporadic visits to Ensenada, some 25 miles distant, he succeeded in making substantial contributions to the explosive population growth of that hamlet. A contingent of his offspring and their families threw a Sunday birthday bash for him before he died, and the rock walls of the cove were festooned with his clan of Anglo-Mexicans, hanging on tight, drinking beer and celebrating the astonishing longevity of their patriarch.

I counted dozens.

He was quite a man.

Even in his waning years, Kennedy was always helpful and kind to the "sport" divers, though he watched them carry away his livelihood in overloaded gunny sacks.

He loved to sip beer and chat, usually speaking in a funny half-English half-Spanish patois. He had actually forgotten most of his English but he seemed to enjoy trying to practice it again.

When Kennedy was younger, the few campesinos roundabout called him "El Tiburon" — The Shark. He could free-dive to 60 feet and work hard for three or four minutes without surfacing. The physical results were a huge barrel chest (to accommodate his diver's lungs) and close-to-paralytic arthritis from the constant exposure to the icy waters of the cove, which due to upwelling were far below normal temperatures.

When I last saw the old man, he could barely shuffle from the pallet in the tiny back room of his shack to the front door where he had greeted so many guests over the years, a distance, perhaps, of eight feet.

Shortly before he died, nearly a decade ago, Kennedy made me a gift of a large and ancient hatch cover he had once towed from the sea. He had been using it as a floor in his outhouse. It had supported me often during our beer-drinking sessions, and having not much else of any notable dimensions to gaze upon during those reflective moments in Kennedy's outhouse, I often found myself staring down covetously at the antiquitous hatch cover.

I had only to mention once that I should like to make a table of it someday and it was mine.

"*El Viejo* must have known the end was near," Mamacita said a week later at the funeral service, half smile, half tears. "But..."

"But what, Mama?" I intoned sadly when she paused.

I was choked up myself.

"Perhaps with an outhouse floor," she said, elbowing me in the ribs and laughing aloud, "he could have lasted one more week."

THE HAIRCUT PLACE

Thanks to my philosophy lessons from Mamacita, I am of the opinion that life is only as complicated as we make it, and if we want to make it complicated enough we can wind up in the looney-tune factory endlessly stitching therapy moccasins.

That is why I nearly always get my hair harvested in Baja, rather than in one of the expensive and confusing tonsorial parlors north of the border. Things are still uncomplicated in rural Baja. I don't have to look at the "Styles Available" pictures on the barber shop wall to decide whether I want the "Executive," the "Ivy League" or the "Sport" look. Making decisions like that has always made me crazy. In Baja, very few barbers even ask whether you want your hair cut short or long, much less offer to shape, style, tease, frizz, shingle or bob it. What they do is simply cut one's hair, making all the decisions themselves as they go along.

I have always admired the simplicity of this approach, and so far it has kept me out of the shoe-stitching biz.

The Baja barber shop can be identified by the sign "Peluqueria," "Barberia" or "Barber Shop," depending on how fussy the owner is about sticking to the Spanish dictionary, and one can always spot the shop from a distance by its universal red and white stripes. Sometimes, in Baja, the owner cannot afford a regular barber pole, so the stripes will simply be painted on the front door or window. But they will always be red and white.

I do not pretend to know the exact origin of these barber colors, but I point to the fact that the red stripes on the American flag, as well as the international symbol of the Red Cross, are both, I believe, meant to be reminiscent of blood, and I see no reason to think less sanguine thoughts when it comes to glimpsing the age-old symbol of the physician/haircutter, the barber pole.

I always think of a haircut as minor surgery, anyway.

I nearly lost an ear one time in a shop called "Benny's" in Beaumont, Texas, when a size-12 trollop sashayed by, wearing a size-9 blouse, just as Benny was about to carve me a new set of sideburns.

I suspect that Benny's is closed now (by order of the Texas Board of Physicians and Surgeons, I should think), but Benny's should more rightly have been called "The Butcher Shop" or, more simply, "Van Gogh's," and I would have thought it appropriate had there been a large stuffed ear mounted conspicuously on the wall somewhere between the Playboy table and the hat rack.

My hair-raising experiences with barbers have not been limited to the U.S.A., however. Baja has given me its share of trauma.

I fell asleep once in a chair in Ensenada, and the barber, not wanting to disturb me, just kept snipping away. When I finally came to, and the guy held the mirror up, my cranium looked like a bruised, sorter-rejected Santa Clara peach.

I am sad to report that in the last year or so my regular Baja barber of nearly five years has taken to strong drink and has set my teeth to grinding when he opens a straight razor. Even his pals rather darkly call him "*El Temblor*." So last week I went scouting for a practitioner with keener eye and steadier hand.

My search led me to what I think may be the ultimate Baja barber shop and, at the very least, the Charlie Chaplin of barbers. The guy's name is Alfonso, and he is a one-man circus.

At nine the other morning, in the little farm town near our place, Alfonso waddled along the dusty business-frontage road adjacent to the highway, brandishing a small paper shopping sack emblazoned "The Golden Door." For those of you who are not familiar with the Golden Door, it is a very posh, $2500-a-week Southern California fat farm where movie stars go to have their corporal carburetors adjusted. I immediately sensed correctly that Alfonso, with such chutzpah, was going to be good for laughs.

Without a word, he nodded good morning to me, unlocked the front door of the dilapidated wooden shack that served as his shop, and launched into 20 minutes of prime Mack Sennett barber business.

With a barber's whisk brush, he deftly flicked a fly off his spotless shirt, then donned a delightfully disreputable, stained-and-spattered white jacket and did two full minutes toying with a single remaining button that was precariously attached to the garment by one thread.

Now, with mock pride, he silently feather dusted an eye-catching collection of large-and-lifelike, wiggly rubber models of bugs (some six inches long) which were mounted on the wall behind the tattered barber chair — a grasshopper, a louse, a cockroach, a weevil, a tarantula, etc. I don't know where the hell he had purchased these fascinating mini-monsters, but there was a strong implication from his expression as he went about the dusting that all of the creatures had been combed from the tresses of his farmer clientele. The bugs were (Alfonso would tacitly have one believe) his trophies.

After the dusting, he did a short shtick with a coffee pot, then threw in a passable routine with a broom, meticulously sweeping up yesterday's hair from the floor and tossing it out the back door with exaggerated ceremony.

Finally, he stepped back and inspected my head like Michelangelo surveying a chunk of Carrara marble. He peered at me, artist style, through a little frame he made with his fingers. He fondled my ears and checked the thickness of my hair by rubbing against the nap, like Arnie Palmer sizing up the ninth green at Pebble Beach.

When the show was all over, Alfonso unceremoniously cut my hair.

He charged only a buck for all this.

A buck!

The haircut, of course, was a basic, uncomplicated defoliation, just as I knew it would be, requiring absolutely no decisions about style on my part. Practically *designed* to keep me out of moccasin therapy.

And sure enough, I haven't had a full-fledged delusion or hallucination since.

Well, some little stuff, maybe. You know. Bugs and such.

But nothing really big.

THE HAPPINESS BOYS

The following event could not transpire today, of course, because the La Paz Police department (in Southern Baja) has undoubtedly cleaned up its act. I am dead certain that all LPPD officers now wear halos and wings, and that they genuflect each morning to *El Jefe* (The Chief) before going about the day's activities, dispensing justice with as even a hand as the Napoleonic Code will allow. Ahem.

However...

Many years back there was at least one freelance, ostensibly on the La Paz force, who outdid even the famous New York horse-patrolman Ignatius Loyola Riley, the glib blackguard who used to sell the nags that were in his charge to unsuspecting tourists, and who divested the City of New York of seventeen eminently serviceable steeds before his epaulets were whisked away by an enraged police commissioner.

In the La Paz caper, I refer specifically to the rogue I shall call Luis de la Mancha, who, with his manservant (an irascible little shyster named Pepe), once tilted at *my* windmill with not a little fervor and more than a modicum of success.

Pepe and Luis saw me coming.

One evening early in the '60s I was driving around that lovely city in a brand new Buick, fecklessly glancing at my watch and trying to guess the exact minute at which I would lose my first fender, when I came upon the Carnaval parade.

Now, in La Paz, as in Mazatlan and Vera Cruz, Carnaval (the Latin equivalent of Mardi Gras) is an occasion of considerable celebration and merriment. It draws a hell of a crowd. Traffic was at a standstill on the clogged thoroughfare I had selected for my evening spin, so in a moment of passionate hysteria I followed the lead of a sensible-looking businessman in the VW in front of me and avoided the traffic by wheeling down a dimly lit alleyway. The VW fellow, I concluded, seemed to have made the transition with reasonable success, having disappeared into the darkness several blocks down the alley, so I felt that the path was a suitable escape route.

At the end of the first block, I was just gathering speed when I detected (out of the corner of my eye) a single headlight from an ancient and battered Chevrolet parked in a side street I was about to pass.

Before I could hit the brakes, the Cyclopean Chevy lurched forward with dazzling acceleration and dismantled the very fender of my earlier conjecture.

I realize, dear reader, that you might not be of age to recall the famous old-time radio show called "Fibber McGee and Molly." The high point of that silliness was always the moment McGee opened the door of a closet loosely stuffed with the accumulated paraphernalia of a lifetime. The sound effects were a challenge to the studio sound man, and he never failed to please the audience by producing crashes, tunks, clunks and tintinnabulations of such delectable variety and volume that one would think a gym locker full of china, cymbals and gongs had just fallen down a flight of stairs.

Such was the effect when Pepe hit my Buick.

By the time my pride-and-joy Buick had spun to a halt and I looked back, the last of Pepe's hub caps was in the final throes of revolutionary *dénouement*, like a giant quarter gyrating to rest on a tin-roofed echo chamber. Around the hub caps on the pavement was an astonishing collection of bumpers, fenders, headlamps, a hood ornament and three door handles — the latter being of extraordinary interest to me since the Chevy had only two doors. I remember wondering how fortunate I was, given the dimension of the cataclysm, that the buildings around us were still intact. There was certainly little left of Pepe's original contraption.

Pepe had no need to open his car door. It was already several yards away from the *débâcle*, so he

88

simply slid off the rump-sprung driver's seat and went directly into his act.

First he fell to the ground, writhing in splendid agony, like an octopus stuck by a pin. When he had thus suffered a respectable period of time, he arose unsteadily and gazed glumly at me with woebegone eyes, shaking his head in despair.

"Oh, señor," he whimpered, now holding his head to keep it from falling off, "you have ruined me. This car, she is all I have in the world, and you have destroyed her."

He peered dolefully at the wreckage.

"How much?" I queried, wishing to dispatch with the folderol I could see coming.

Pepe was surprised by the alacrity of my decision to be sensible, and a hint of a grin breezed across his face. Then he dropped to the ground and started drawing imaginary numbers on the pavement, occasionally glancing back over his shoulder at the sundry car parts to more accurately determine their replacement value.

I suddenly realized that this was not going to be an insignificant scam. Pepe was working on getting a totally new car out of the deal.

The fact that Pepe had hit me, rather than vice versa, was inconsequential, of course. By Mexican law, in an accident of this sort the participants usually either settle on the spot, provide proof of valid Mexican insurance or go directly to jail without passing Go, to await adjudication by a municipal judge. Since my insurance had run out the day previous, I had it figured that my only alternative to the hoosegow was to slip Pepe a few bucks and take my lumps, but his finger-drawn figures were mounting frightfully.

Then Luis appeared.

He was the most impeccably attired Mexican policeman I have ever seen, rigged out with medals and stars and all sorts of ribbons which would lead one to believe he was at the least an Argentine *general*, and possibly the beamed-down commander of a more esoteric, inter-galactic force, though he was hiding behind a pair of handcuffs which I perceived to be the size of hula hoops, thus amply signifying that he was a law man, not a true military man. In either case, the overall effect was one of unquestionable authority.

The cuffs appeared to be of the same sturdy alloy as bank-vault doors and had an enormous keyhole for which I was certain no key had ever been made.

"*Buenas noches*, señor," he said, brushing at an imaginary mote on the braid of his sleeve. "What a fine evening for Carnaval, eh?"

"Yes, officer," I rejoined, "and what brings you this way?"   In Mexico, of course, no one ever gets immediately to the business of business, but my response was perhaps a bit too frivolous vis-à-vis the disaster before us, and Luis' jaunty air of camaraderie changed drastically.

The Notebook came out.

"Hmmm. What do we have here, señor?" he said sternly, surveying the incredible breadth of the fiasco. "A very serious difficulty, I see. Insurance?" "No. No insurance. How much for the damage?" I was anxious to establish quickly whether I was going to jail or Pepe would be satisfied with what was in my wallet.

"Well, let me see, señor," the general said, nudging a crumpled bumper with a well-polished Sonoran riding boot. "This is very serious. You have done very important damage to this man's car." He glanced down at Pepe, who was still drawing numbers the pavement. "How much did you pay for this fine Chevrolet, my good man?"

Pepe rattled off a figure which might as well have been a million dollars.

"That much, eh?" said Luis. He shook his jowls at me Nixon-style. "Well, well, señor. This is very serious. I am afraid that unless you have the money, we will have to go to the jail."

With that he reached for the bank-vault handcuffs.

"Thirty dollars," I said, making an offer I knew would be refused.

"Two hundred," Luis countered.

Little Pepe writhed and rubbed his neck.

The rest is history. Dickering is dickering, no matter where one does it, and though this exchange was of some intricacy and included many fine typically Mexican negotiating ploys ("This poor man, whom you have now further impoverished, has only a dirt home and a cat, and the cat has but two legs"; "His cupboard lacks frijoles and his mice have the look of death"), the session was no more exhausting than what one would expect on a hometown used-car lot in the U.S.A.

In the end I handed Pepe a wad of pesos worth approximately $70.

Pepe counted the money very slowly, with a good deal of grumbling that the amount was far below his expectations, then routinely handed half to Luis.

Luis smiled. I smiled. And the two old pals began searching the debris for the loose bits of wire and string with which they would reassemble the wondrous breakaway Chevy for the next exciting run at a terrifically easy mark.

FAMOUS ANIMALS
I HAVE KNOWN

If you happen to be planning an extended visit to the countryside in Baja, or you are thinking of retiring to one of the many rural tourist/retirement communities along Baja's west coast, there is something you should know.

The place is crawling with animals.

Campo Loco is only 25 minutes from busy Ensenada, yet our sophisticated city guests are always terribly disappointed to find that they must rise from their slumber at dawn because that's when the real world wakes up.

The symphony starts with Mamacita's roosters, moves forward with the rhythmic bass croak of a frog that lives somewhere under our bedroom floor, gathers force with the chatter of the swallows, and climaxes with the thousand violins of the cicadas.

It is also at this time of day that the screech owl makes his last pass by our bedroom window, the first quail begin calling, and the seagulls start crying on the sea cliff in front of the casa, where they expect me to clean fish 24 hours a day.

This is all particularly bothersome to me. As if the noise were not enough, worry drives me from my bed.

You see, I know that the *silent* hordes are out there.

Every morning, waves of cottontails come for breakfast in our garden.

Cottontails are terrible pests. They will not touch the geraniums, bougainvillea, nasturtiums, or petunias which practically grow wild here. But every time we plant something new and exotic from one of the high-priced plant boutiques, some traffic-directing jackrabbit out there sounds assembly, and the multitudes are upon us.

I once asked Miguel Lopez' mother, who always seems to have baskets of fresh produce in her kitchen, and whose flower garden is a wonder, how she grows any crops at all with the rabbits around.

Her answer was very direct, very practical and very Mexican. "Plant enough for the rabbits."

My rabbits have become bold as organ-grinder monkeys, and they do all the tricks except tip their hats as they munch.

Not only do my rabbits display fearlessness in my presence, they intimidate me by feigning total disinterest.

They will eat a sweetpea tendril to the nub while I stamp my foot. They will demolish the choicest verbena while I wave my arms like a whirligig. Though I heartily enjoy an occasional rabbit stew when El Coyote comes by with a rifle to thin the bunny population, I cannot bring myself to shoot our little wretches myself, since I know so many of them by name (Diana, Mazeppa, Tokyo Rose, etc.). Our place, Coyote claims, is the Kenya of this continent as far as rabbit hunting goes.

I have essayed other ways to get rid of the rabbits besides turning Coyote loose. I have tried plastic netting (which they eat through), poison (which they don't eat through), and all kinds of traps (which they smile at and bypass).

I have tried everything short of land mines on my rabbits, with little effect. They seem to know the Number One Rabbit Lesson very well, so there are more of them every year.

Our two house dogs (Clancy and Taco) don't lose any sleep worrying about rabbits. When the dogs finally wake up, they have a little game of running the rabbits off hippety-hop, but with not much enthusiasm. Our dogs are not intent, intrepid hunters, ever-vigilant. They were bred to sleep and to eat little round pellets of doggy junk food that costs $4.98 a sack, plus "Cheweez," and "Bonz," both of which run about the same price as top sirloin.

Every time Sylvia fills the dog dish, I die a little.

Yesterday I asked Sylvia why our dogs could not get their Cheweez and Bonz off the flanks of the long-eared dispose-alls that whir around in our garden. "It wouldn't be the same," she said mysteriously.

The other plague upon our house is *topos* — gophers.

Let me tell you, there are 17 guaranteed ways to get rid of gophers, and none of them works. The best one can hope to do to stem the tide is to push pins into little gopher dolls.

Carlos Jimenez, a local farmer, once told me that the *topos* **own** Baja. He says that the burrows of the Baja gophers are so well interconnected that a gopher could eat the bottom off a carrot in Tijuana and burp 700 miles away in Cabo San Lucas without once coming up for air.

There are other animals around, too.

When the coyotes start yipping on the hillside behind our casa (especially on full-mooned, hot summer nights) my wife and I herd Clancy and Taco into the protection of the living room before they become dog food, *real* dog food, for the predators.

And one night, after returning home to find that I had left a door ajar, I came upon a very large skunk in the kitchen, curled up in our king-sized glass cookie jar, sated on an entrée of ginger snaps.

Domesticated animals in Baja also become adept and fearless scroungers.

There is a scruffy-looking mongrel in our camp, for example, who will snatch a sizzling steak off a white-hot barbecue the instant one's back is turned.

But our champion scrounger of all times was Kojak.

Kojak was an antic camp pig who used to promenade with the local pack of pups and often had to be shooed out of the house.

Like most animals around camp — this includes the twin goats that leveled our tomatoes and *calabasas*, the one-eyed feral cat that has found a home among the mice in our woodshed, and the spotted calf that ate our morning glories — Kojak simply appeared one day. He was a mere piglet the size of a (God forgive me) football, squeaking and squealing in pre-adolescent pig language.

We all learned later that he had actually been acquired by Mamacita's son, through a swap of two treadless 7 X 15 Goodyear tires and a J. C. Penney battery that might or might not have taken one more charge.

Kojak soon chewed his way through the delicious hemp rope which tethered him to a horseshoe stake. He celebrated his freedom by calling on each home in camp, sniffing around front and back doors, seeking out hiding places beneath porches, and generally familiarizing himself with what was to become his piggy domain.

Unlike most pigs (I think), Kojak could dance. He would prance and pirouette, lifting all fours off the ground when offered food. And folks flocked in from miles around when Kojak lapsed into his *tours jetés*.

He was particularly fond of watermelon and would do a sort of Gene Kelly thing or a jig whenever he saw Sylvia approaching with a bucket of watermelon rinds.

The poor little bugger subsisted for nearly two years on the meager table scraps of half a dozen

Mexican and gringo families in the neighborhood. He became terribly excited at the prospect of food (often, I must admit with some embarrassment, wetting on the spot).

There is no denying it. Kojak was a comic. A porcine Cantinflas. But the little bastard was a terrible thief.

One Fourth of July our fishing companion and resident accordionist, Roberto the Music Man, had prepared five kilos of *carne asada* for our annual summer fiesta. The spicy beef had been marinated until it could be sliced with a whisper, and the night before the big day it was carefully locked away in an ice chest with a twisting, window-type lock. The chest, in turn, was cautiously stowed away beneath the Music Man's camper in our driveway, so that under no circumstance could the lid be lifted.

These heady precautions did not deter Kojak. The fact is, they seemed to present something of a challenge to the little porker, and he reacted admirably to the thrown gauntlet.

Not only was Kojak able to hustle the chest out from under the camper, but he succeeded in twisting open the lock.

When we found the discarded chest in the morning, it had a freshly scrubbed look to it. There was nary a lick of marinade. Not a morsel of meat. Not a spot of refuse. Not a smidgeon of onion or chile or blood or juice.

It was more immaculate than when new.

To cap the achievement, Kojak had also lifted the

heavy, rock-covered lid off a giant iron pot of *elotes* — 24 ears of corn.

The landscaping, the patio, the garden, the driveway, all were littered with corn husks. The scene was like the edge-of-town site of some mad, drunken husking bee.

Even the petunias and portulacas had been trampled flat in the glee of the exercise.

The culprit was nowhere to be found.

Kojak, we surmised, was lolling in some kind of pig Heaven, where trees hang heavy with watermelon rinds and where kitchen doors are always left open.

Then, from the arroyo, 50 feet from the scene of the crime, we heard a faint grunt. Investigation revealed Kojak, on his side, his little legs thrust outward like the detonators on a sea mine, his beloved curlicue tail twitching autonomically at an occasional fly. Breathing came in short bursts. He was smiling dazedly. *Smiling.*

But what was most memorable were his long, blond eyelashes — everyone agreed they were his best feature — now half closed, fluttering just perceptibly in fleeting convulsions of masochistic ecstasy.

Kojak lay there the better part of the day. He only pattered off late in the afternoon when the pregnant black German shepherd, Osa, nuzzled him awake, presumably to see if her old pal were still alive.

The following day, Mamacita hobbled down the

hill to invite the gang of us to her casa.

"I have a *sorpresa*," she said mysteriously.

When we arrived, of course, we all wanted to see the suprise immediately, but Mama stalled.

"No, no. Later," she said, brushing at a wisp of hair. Then she passed around the guacamole, filled everyone's beer glasses, even went to the kitchen for a tray of steaming tamales.

"Delicious," the Music Man opined, tongueing the tiny harmonica around in his mouth along with an olive pit. "Never tasted better. What's in 'em?"

"*Pato de Culiacan*," Mama answered with the Sad Indian look. "Culiacan duck."

Then she retired to the kitchen, where she stayed for a very long time.

In Baja it is impolite to laugh aloud at the expense of one's guests.

'TILL DEATH DO US PART

The American retirement communities in Baja fairly burst with dingbats who march to different drummers.

Mr. Dimmick is one. He's a guy who always seems to be in some kind of difficulty.

Dimmick — "The first name's Theophilus, but (self-conscious chuckle) you can call me Ted" — is a tall, skinny, disaster-prone nebbish who always has a story about his latest Baja "troubles," usually told in a monotone with sad resigned eyes and long reflective pauses. He has taken to plastering his sparse strands of dyed-black hair down on his dome with some kind of goo, though I remember him when his follicles were more bountiful. This, combined with his excessive Adam's apple, his paucity of flesh and a certain rolling gait, gives him the appearance of a semi-bald Ichabod Crane.

The way Dimmick explained one of his mishaps to me was this: His wife had invited her mother, a lady of some 80 summers, to visit the Dimmicks' Baja home for a week. After a rough trip down from Los Angeles, the old woman was feeling puny for the first few days, and even worse after that.

In fact, she had a massive heart attack and died.

Now, if you're a gringo (or, in this case, a *gringa*) you don't want to die in Baja.

The paperwork is all in triplicate.

It is altogether a very sticky business.

Mr. Dimmick, being a Baja resident for some years, knew all about that, which is probably why he did what he did. He simply neglected to tell anyone in Mexican officialdom about the demise of the old girl. Instead, he very carefully placed the body in a large green sleeping bag, zipped it up, and strapped the whole shebang to the top of his station wagon.

The problem, now, was to get the body through U.S. Customs. Dimmick's wife stayed home, too upset to argue about his unconventional modus operandi.

Dimmick pulled up to the Customs gate with a smile. Over the years he had learned that a smile was the best weapon to use in the border war.

It worked.

A young officer with curly blond hair and fuzzy cheeks peered briefly under a front fender, kicked a tire, and merely grunted at the lumpy green bag on the roof. On the OK-to-pass signal, Dimmick took off so fast he nearly whiplashed himself.

He buzzed up the freeway till he came to the big shopping center in San Ysidro, where he planned to call a mortician friend and tell him about the silent passenger above decks.   Dimmick was upset, naturally. The worry of the border crossing was past, but he was still somewhat shaken by the whole experience, and he cursed under his breath as he cruised around the Safeway parking lot without finding an empty parking space.

Finally, after he had made three turns through the lot, a little blue Volkswagen eased out of a slot just eight spaces from the public pay phone. Dimmick pulled into the space slowly, so as not to further jar the body, took a small book of addresses and phone numbers from his breast pocket and jingled the coins he had carefully loaded in the little zipper-pocket on his jacket. Always a stickler for detail, his planning so far had been perfect. He had even brought along an extra can of gasoline so he would not have to stop at a station where some nosy attendant might start asking about the supercargo.

Then, just as he was about to head toward the empty phone booth, a large Mexican woman, dragging a cranky child, jammed herself and her kid into the booth, puffing to get the door shut.

Dimmick sat silently in the front seat, drumming his fingers against the face of his Bulova. He had come this far, he could wait another few minutes. He watched with irritation as the fat woman gesticulated while talking, nearly punching her fist through the glass panel behind the phone.

She talked for 25 minutes, and as she emerged, pushing the squealing child ahead of her, Dimmick sprinted toward the booth.

He rummaged for the change, set the nickels, dimes and quarters in neat stacks on the little steel shelf, and prepared to call the mortician's number.

As Dimmick's bony finger pushed the buttons, a young man wearing a fringed buckskin coat, leaning against an electric rocking horse in front of the market, stared intently at him.

The boy had a sallow complexion and a drooping left eye. Dimmick would remember that later when making out the police report.

Slowly the boy sauntered over to the station wagon. Then he jumped in and drove away.

Just drove away.

That was three years ago.

The police have never found the station wagon or Mr. Dimmick's mother-in-law.

The whole incident, Dimmick says, shaking his head sorrowfully, has placed considerable strain on his marital relationship.

WATSON COME HERE, I NEED YOU

Alexander Graham Bell's great invention has at last come to Baja.

Actually, the first few phones were put in at Tijuana in the early '30s, but today the phone book for this city of more than a million is still less than an inch thick. It takes two to three years to get a phone installed after ordering it, and until 1980 there was no direct dialing into the *Frontera*. Because of the enormous population growth, exchange equipment is outmoded before it is installed, and phone service in Baja has always been less than adequate. Wags refer to the Mexican phone company as "Taco Bell."

Until recently, one had to go directly to the phone company to make a long-distance call, and this could entail a wait of as much as several hours as the office was usually crowded with would-be callers or the circuits were all busy.

The telephone problem still drives Baja business-men wild, and gringos, used to semi-efficient Ma Bell, just shake their heads in disbelief.

Most Baja operators are bilingual, which makes things a little easier for the gringos, but there never seem to be enough operators to handle the calls. Often, an operator will politely ask what number you want, then mysteriously click off, only to come bouncing back five minutes later, asking again for the number.

CB and microwave radio have substantially filled the communications gap in Baja. There are micro-wave relay stations the length of the peninsula and many Bajans have CB in their home or vehicle. Truckloads of hot CBs were pilfered from Alta California in the '70s and sold in Baja at bargain prices.

The gringo retirement community has a particularly large CB network, especially in the Ensenada area, and for many the CB has become equivalent to the telephone they were used to up north. But on CB, of course, conversations are *broadcast*, and thus open to all ears. There are very few secrets in the Baja CB homes anymore.

One old boy in Campo Loco forgets the party-line characteristic of CB every time he gets sauced up, and he amuses the entire community by calling each of his would-be girl friends in succession, much to the consternation of his understanding wife. It doesn't much amuse the wooees, either, who listen intently to his calls, hoping they will not be next on his call list.

Long-suffering Mexican women, on the other hand, have found CB an excellent way to keep track of errant husbands. The wife often puts pleading children on the wireless to shame the old man into coming home from the saloon. The kids seem to be trained to wail in authentic pain and anguish.

In Baja, CB is far more reliable than telephone service, but its range, of course, is limited to only five or ten miles, so there is no hope of using it for calls to the U.S.

For many years I tried to do business from Ensenada long distance, using the phone. But when wires were down, or there were heavy periods of emergency-calling due to floods and washouts, I simply couldn't get through. Other times there would be the traditional two- or three-hour wait at the phone company, by which time I would forget what I was calling for. Needless to say, my business suffered.

When Percy Hussong was still alive, he used to let me use the private phone in his office at the cantina, but if the call took more than an hour to get through (which it usually did) I was so *geshtunken* on Percy's potent booze that I never made much sense on the phone and promptly lost track of the details anyway.

Some of my stateside contacts were familiar with the rigamarole I had to go through to keep in touch. Others simply couldn't figure out why I wasn't chatting with them several times a day. "Why don't you just pick up the phone once in a while?" was a question I had frequently to answer. I am certain that not one of my clients has ever really believed my explanation. The communications difficulty cost me a lot of business over the years, and calling from Hussong's all the time convinced many clients that my Remington was permanently located in a cantina.

Even when I was on the wagon, my calls from Baja were suspect. One client in particular, an important advertising account executive from whom I was getting considerable freelance business, was about to give up on me after several particularly frenetic moments on the long-distance phone. But I resolved somehow to correct the problem.

As it happened, the little farm community about 10 miles down the road from our casa finally got a phone, located in the village grocery store. With the new facility I pictured my business soaring. In his San Diego office, I promised my concerned account executive that I would religiously call him every day at three to keep him abreast of progress and take any additional instructions. Then I headed back to Baja.

The following afternoon I set out from the casa to make the first call, cold sober, anxious to convince my client that our communications problems were solved.

I was ecstatic. I had the best of all possible worlds. I whistled a Mexican ditty as I drove along the edge of the lagoon on the way to the village, watching the cranes, egrets and sandpipers stalk the shoreline. The day was fine. The corn was high in the fields.

Here and there an Indian family could be seen bending over a row of ripe chiles.

As I rounded the last turn into the village, I did a classic double take. There was festivity in the air. The village was aflurry with activity. Almost oblivious to traffic, people were walking back and forth across the highway that serves as the village's main street. They were gathered in small groups in front of the several little shops, talking animatedly. They were lined up at the *carnitas* and *tamal* stands and clogging the doorway of the village ice cream shop.

A wild-eyed *vaquero* in full, silver-studded *charro* suit, reared back on a huge bay stallion, the mount's forehooves pedaling in the air just above the hood of a traffic-bound yellow Camaro with Saskatchewan license plates. With a whisk of his sombrero on the horse's rump, the cowboy turned the animal, galloped full speed off the highway and disappeared in the dust toward the nearby hills and ranch country from whence he had come.

There were children everywhere, darting in and out among the conversational groups, playing tag, throwing pebbles at each other. Huddled apart in other groups were clusters of Zapotec Indians, chattering in their own tongue. The women, barely four feet tall, were wearing their traditional shirts and skirts of bright turquoise, yellow, red or green, with pants beneath the skirts for their work in the fields.

Now I remembered the reason for the activity in

the village.

Today was *El Dia de los Muertos*, The Day of the Dead, Mexico's universal fiesta day, celebrated by all races in Mexico, including the Indians.

As I got out of my pickup and walked through a group of Zapotecs who barely came up to my navel, my heart sank.

The store with the revered telephone was jammed with shoppers, all talking at the same time. To add to the festivity, the store owner had turned on a radio full blast, and the raucous sound of *Sinaloense* tubas and trap drums rattled the jars of *jalapeños* on the shelves. The decibel count was off the chart.

Then I saw the phone.

It was not in an enclosed booth, but on a candy counter right next to a cash register which was now ringing ferociously at each purchase. A Mexican friend of mine was shouting into the phone hopelessly, as though trying to intimidate a brick wall.

"I can't hear what you are saying," he screamed, "but I am waiting for the bus and I will be in Tijuana tonight!" Then he slammed down the receiver with a choice Baja epithet and muscled through the crowd to the cashier to pay for the call.

Still waiting to call were another Mexican fellow I knew and a gringo neighbor of mine.

I looked at my watch and winced. I had promised to call at three, and it was now 3:15.

By 4:30 the Mexican had finished his call and the gringo had gone home in disgust.

My client would be leaving his office at five, but if I had any luck at all, I would still talk to him the day I said I would, if not the precise hour.

As is customary, I scribbled the phone number on a pad by the phone, and the girl behind the counter placed the call. Half an hour went by before she finally shouted over the crowd.

"Señor! Señor! Your call!"

Just as she said this, two dozen Zapotecs flooded through the front door, highly agitated, waving their arms.

"What's going on?" I asked the girl, holding my hand over the receiver.

The tiny Zapotecs swirled around me like dervishes, bumping, chattering, pushing me into the candy counter.

"They want to buy some candy," the girl shouted. "Someone gave them some pesos and they want to buy some candy!"

By the time I removed my hand from the receiver, the noise had reached an incredible new pitch — blaring music, ringing cash registers, haggling customers, chattering Indians, all going at the same time.

"Hello, Norm?" I said, as loudly as possible without sounding frantic.

"Fred? Fred? What the hell is going on there? Where the hell are you? Are you back in that damned saloon again?"

I gathered my wits as best I could and enunciated very clearly.

"Norm," I said levelly, "I know you are not going to believe this, but I am absolutely sober and I am not in a saloon. I am, however, being attacked by a tribe of sugar-crazed Zapotec Indians and..."

The click on the other end was definitive and final.

FASTEST GUN IN THE WEST

Nothing is so ludicrous to me as a stuffed shirt revealed, and I find plenty to laugh at in Baja because while few stand on ceremony here, when they do they are usually defrocked instantly and with no regret by flinty experts.

Agatha Svensen comes to mind — Aggie, the epitome of what one might call durable goods, a tiny, seasoned woman reminiscent of Barbara Stanwyck in that scrap of television jetsam called *Ponderosa* or *Bar B-Q*, or something like that. Just five feet tall, this sturdy little dust devil is boss lady on one of the biggest *ranchos* in Baja, up in the high country, and she do not cater to no folderol, if'n you know what I mean. She wears jeans, yet is coiffed. Behind the six-irons, Aggie is, essentially, a lady.

The defrockee in this case was a gentleman named Horace Begg, from Hollee-wood, California. But I'll get to him in a minute.

There are a few things you should know about Aggie.

The matched Colts are not cosmetic.

She rides, shoots, and can yank a heifer to the turf in eight seconds while rolling a smoke.

One other snippet of background: It has been my experience that there is a cultural aberration in Mexico which time and again results in difficulties of deplorable magnitude. Little boys are frequently taught by insecure fathers to be bullies. This is the *yang* half of *machismo*, emanating from a de facto matriarchal society.

Try to pull off a tad of this hooliganism on a lady named Aggie, however, and what you get is Popocatapetl volcano on a busy day.

The Svensen Ranch was pioneered by Aggie's now-96-year-old father, Nils, back in the days when revolutionaries, renegade *colorados* and local warlords could be expected to burn the barn at any moment, and Nils and his brothers fought them off on several occasions with Sears Roebuck Winchesters and an elk rifle that used bullets which looked like small fire hydrants.

Nils now lives in a small house a few hundred yards from the *hacienda* and the Svensen boys are scattered throughout Baja, running a variety of enterprises ranging from lobstering to farming.

In the '50s, Aggie and her sister Dagmar chose to stay on at the ranch during hard times, turning it into a fly-in dude operation, catering to rhinestone cowboys, businessmen mostly, from all over the West, who were at heart frustrated bronc riders. The ladies put in a dozen small, rustic, motel-size rooms down by the bunkhouse, built a swimming pool, then cut out the gentlest of the horses to accept the broad rear ends which would soon swoop down out of the skies in their Cessnas and Pipers and Beechcrafts.

One of these big-ass birds was Horace Begg, a "film producer," he said, who emerged from his fire-red Apache at the end of the mountain strip, sniffed the pine-scented air, and actually beat his chest gorilla-fashion, as his playmate, a comedic mound of fluff named Fifi something, put on her makeup in the cockpit for the benefit, only, of a few straggled Herefords which were munching the grass near the apron. The cows took no note, so she pursed her lips and said "Ooooo" to no one in particular.

When Begg's layers of pectoral flab had come to rest — he would actually notice bruises around the nipples later while sucking in his stomach in front of a mirror — the alien couple hopped into a ranch-hand piloted Jeep which had pulled up nose-to-nose with the prop.

The hand, a wiry poke named Tubby, peered right through Begg's corpulence at the starlet's semi-revealed mammaries, then nearly hit a tree on the way back to the *hacienda* due to his attempt to negotiate the winding road while locking his head in the direction from whence he had come.

A Culver City milkshake was being created in the back seat before his very eyes.

This hanky panky did not set well with Begg, and

he spent the rest of his stay posturing and trying to talk like John Wayne.

"Ooooo," Fifi would say, and feel Begg's muscle.

Oh, I could go on and on, I suppose — the saddle sores, the falls in the pig sty, the campfire night when Begg projected himself as one of the Sons of the Pioneers though he sang in a pathetic monotone and spooked the mules... yes, friends, it was all there.

But it was the conclusion of the farce that made the episode worthwhile.

On the last Saturday evening of our hero's stay at the ranch, he had peaked. He had developed a distinct Wayne swagger, dragging his left foot in the dirt as he traversed the rancho's pathways, hand constantly on an imaginary holster, pausing only to push his movie-lot cowboy hat to the back of his head and to survey the horizon with wise, narrowed eyes.

Aggie was at the point of dressing some of the hands as Indians and sending them up to the north ridge on ponies just to scare the hell out of Horace, when a seventeen-year-old Mexican boy beat her to the punch.

Eight of us were seated around the dining room table in the main house gorging ourselves on barbecued beef and fresh groceries just picked from the garden, when there was a stir in the kitchen. One of the Mexican girls, muffling a scream, came bursting out of the big ranch-style kitchen, pointing speechlessly behind her.

Horace figured one of the girls had burned herself, or perhaps seen a mouse.

"Don't worry, Ag," he Wayned, rising from his chair and patting the phantasmic firearm, "I'll see to it."

By now, his foot was dragging so pronouncedly he nearly tripped on the way to the kitchen door.

Aggie instinctively knew the problem was more serious than mice and rose herself to investigate. She had difficulty getting by Horace. He was frozen in the doorway. His paunch had gone slack, his jaw had dropped, his legs were of equal length.

"My God," he quavered, "he's got a gun." He looked back at the group around the table and whispered dully, "He's got a gun. A real gun."

"What's going on?" Aggie barked, and pushed the gelatinous Horace aside. "What the hell do *you* want?" we heard her say, and all rose to peek through the doorway, pushing Horace ahead of us, though he was desperately trying to go the other way, like someone trying to get through a subway door before the exiting crowd thinned.

At the screen door at the back of the kitchen stood a young man clad in a dusty army uniform, a vintage carbine clutched to his chest.

"Señora," the boy snapped angrily, "I am going to inspect your house. Open this latch!" He tapped the butt of the rifle on the door frame.

Aggie stood in the center of the kitchen, hands fisted at her narrow waist. She did not wear her hardware at dinner, favoring a skirt and sweater, so

117

she posed no immediate threat to the boy.

"You are going to *what*?" she exploded.

"Come. Open up," the boy persisted, banging on the door. He took a step backward and pointed the rifle at Aggie's midsection. Fifi screamed.

"Open up or I will have to shoot you all," the boy growled, and snapped the bolt shut on the weapon.

This, friends, is a no-no anywhere in the world. It is particularly bad judgment on the Svensen ranch in Baja California in the presence of Agatha Svensen.

She stalked straight at the muzzle. "Who the hell sent you?" she demanded through the screen, with misleading coolness.

"*Mi Sargento*," the boy said, backing off another step and pointing the gun slightly off to one side.

"And what does your *Sargento* want you to do in my house?" Aggie said, in splinters of brittle steel.

"Investigate," the boy mumbled, shuffling back a few more inches. "We are investigating all the ranchos for marijuana. I have orders."

"*Cabron!*" Aggie erupted and tore at the screen door, ripping out the latch hook. She took one giant step forward for womankind and grabbed the stunned soldier's rifle, in one arc, throwing it to the kitchen floor. Then she reached up and grasped the boy's ears, pulling his beardless face to hers.

"Now, you little turd of a goat," she whispered through grated teeth, "you get back to your *Sargento*, and tell him that Aggie Svensen has your gun. It is government property, I am sure. He will want it

118

back. And he will want you, I think, back in your crib. Go now! Tell him to come with his nicest apology."

With that the terror-stricken boy turned and ran, tears in his eyes, up the leaf-strewn road toward an army vehicle, its motor running, parked in front of the bunkhouse.

"Come," Aggie said, smiling and turning to wipe her hands on one of the frightened girls' aprons. "Let's finish dinner."

Horace was not among us.

In the distance we could just make out the cough and sputter of an Apache, its plugs starting to fire on a regular basis.

"Ooooo," said Fifi, sitting down to her summer squash with a devilish smile, "has anyone seen Tubby?"

THE YULE FROG

Christmas always reminds me of the town dump in Hingham, Massachusetts.

Years ago, the men of Hingham used to gather there every Sunday morning to get rid of the week's trash, have a few beers and make football bets. Everybody showed up, from the big corporate executives to the town street sweeper. It was something of a tribal council. As a result of these meetings, most of the men of Hingham knew one another. It got to be more or less of a social obligation to appear at the dump. "Get well soon" cards were perfunctorily sent to absentees.

Wives used to ask "What on earth do you *do* all that time at the dump, John?" John would puff on his pipe with a wistful faraway look and grunt, "What's for dinner?"

It drove the women nuts. They imagined all sorts of paranoid things. Belly dancers coming out of cakes. Dirty movies. Secret trysts with a mistress. I don't know. Whatever women think about.

(Men have their own infidelity fantasies, which I think are different.)

Anyway, one Christmas the boys got to decorating a scrawny little Christmas tree with bits of trash and their empty beer cans. The branches were festooned with chains of pop-top rings. By Christmas Day you could scarcely find the tree for the decorations.

The next year the tree was a little bigger. And the next year, bigger still. Pretty soon it was a 30-foot blue spruce, and the guys were taking a real interest in it. It was a pop-art spectacular.

The tree got to looking so good that one Christmas they invited all the wives to come and see it. The sight of the tree dispelled the ladies' curiosity, and for several years following, dump paranoia and gossip came almost to a standstill.

These were three or four banner years for the philanderers in the group because they had an open track. They eventually got caught, of course, when the tree-trimming excuse wore out. The wives were furious when they realized they had been hoodwinked after all.

But to get to the point, whimsy in art has always fascinated me. And nobody is as good at it as the Mexican. it is a natural resource of Mexico. A national asset.

A Mexican can take the simplest throwaway item and create something of interest, if not an *objet d'art*. The Aztecs were weaving museum-piece tapestries entirely of feathers long before the Europeans ever figured out what feathers were for.

But more often than not, native Mexican craftsmen choose whimsical subjects for their creations. One cannot visit the most remote village without finding some sort of joke a local Andy Warhol has played on the viewer.

In a tiny beach encampment near Bahia Magdalena, I once saw a life-size statue of a burro made entirely of the dry dung of that animal, held together by chicken wire.

Almost all animals make good subjects, but there are certain persistent themes. Owls are very big with the folk artists. I have seen owls made of sea shells, sticks, pebbles, palm fronds, broken glass, bits of junk metal, corn husks, hair and even human teeth.

Fish, songbirds, deer, roosters, and pigs are also popular subjects, and all lend themselves to humorous treatment of one sort or other.

But it you took a poll among Mexico's artisans, the funniest thing in nature is the frog. You can really do a frog justice by fashioning it of oddball materials.

Mexican folk artists seem to think that the very funniest thing to make a pop-art frog out of is a *real* frog. What you do is taxiderm the damned thing in a sitting or standing position and stick a miniature violin in its hands (or its claws, or whatever those things are). You want funny? This is FUNNY.

In Tijuana, I once saw a lady from Boston go rubber-legged at a window display of a bullfrog playing a violin. Then her husband got in a fight with her on the street for being "over-civilized." *That* was funny. So the beat goes on with stuffed frogs. Kind of a running gag.

There is a mysterious Mexican folk artist loose in Baja who makes "rock frogs." That is, he paints rocks to look like frogs. Big rocks. Boulders, sometimes five or six feet high. They turn out to be very big frogs.

Vaudevillian Pappy O'Toole nearly shut down his vodka distillery because of this comedian. "I was just passing Bajamar, 60 miles an hour," Pappy told me, "when I see this big frog ahead on the roadside, getting ready to jump. Honest to God, pal, the critter must have gone five hundred pounds."

Then he held his glass up to the sunlight. "That's the first bad batch I've had in twenty years," he added sadly.

That was some years ago. I notice lately that there is also a rock frog at San Miguelito. I don't know if the artist is the same one who did the Bajamar frog, though. The painting technique is different. More spots. At any rate, I would guess that these two frogs do more to deter drinking drivers than any billboard campaign the government could mount.

The frog artist gets out and paints his Bajamar frog at Christmastime every year. The fellow has pride.

I picture him on that distant plain, in the dead of night, hoisting a lone toast of Christmas cheer, roaring in merriment at the far-off squeal of brakes and the tentative blowing of a horn.

I hope he will not get too cocky and reveal to a troubled wife where he is going on those full-mooned Santa Claus nights with such a gleam in his eye, paint buckets akimbo, brushes held high. I know from Hingham days that his wife will eventually go for that frog story with a tortilla skillet when he comes reeling home one night in gleeful triumph.

THE MAN BEHIND THE FROG

(After writing the preceding chapter, I was asked by the Baja Times to interview the mysterious Frog Man of Baja. This is the article as it appeared.)

I have found him — the phantom artist who paints Baja's giant roadside boulders to look like frogs or birds or whatever strikes his fancy.

The mysterious Frog Man of Baja.

I went after him with the zeal of a Stanley for a Livingston. Like John Reed looking for Pancho Villa.

I must admit I expected to find a joke of a man. A comic. A blithe spirit. A whimsical creature with Marty Feldman eyes and a fright wig. Someone I could have fun exposing in the style of a caricature. A great laugh.

I did not expect to find this man Acosta.

Perhaps I should tell you how I found him. It was through a tip from the editor of the Baja Times, who said, "He works at the Foreign Book in Ensenada. I am sure of it."

The Foreign Book is in a room the size of a roller rink, right next to the alabaster Riviera Pacifico Hotel, whose Moorish parapets flank the inner harbor of the great half-moon bay called Bahia Todos

Santos, the Bay of All Saints.

The betting room reminds me of a Greyhound bus station I once slept in when I was hitchhiking someplace in southern Georgia. Something out of William Faulkner.

This day there were more employees in the place than customers. One small group of bettors, between postings of race results, watched an old black-and-white Cantinflas movie on a 19-inch Sony mounted high in one corner of the hazy room. Cantinflas was playing cards with a man and a woman. The scene kept shifting from the comic's innocent face to his feet beneath the table, where he was stepping on the man's toes. The day's winners in the motley audience laughed. The losers watched sullenly.

A Chinese man, old and hunched, shuffled over from a betting window to rejoin the group. As he approached them, counting his change, he talked to himself with considerable animation — a peculiarity which the regulars ignored.

A stout, decaying Mexican woman, who appeared destitute, smoked a cigar. Havana, I would guess by the size of it. Two dollars.

A youngish, pockmarked gringo, with unkempt strings of long blond hair and a leg that ended at the knee, played with his aluminum crutch and stared with eyes dull as unwashed grapes at a tote board — Viet Nam?

The tote boards run the length of one wall of the room. At the top of three of the boards, in very large

126

letters, are printed: AQUEDUCT...
LAUREL...HOLLYWOOD PARK.

There is a narrow ramp at the base of these boards. One man is at the far end of this ramp with two buckets of water and a large sponge. He is wiping yesterday away in practiced arcs. There is not a chalk mark left. Not a broken dream. The board glistens.

Closer on the ramp, a slim, neatly dressed, middle-aged Mexican with a small salt-and-pepper mustache and horn-rimmed glasses is very rapidly hand-lettering the day's entries from Maryland. He looks a little like Mister Rogers.

The letters are perfectly drawn and spaced, block style, but with an indefinable character of their own — microcosmic signatures of the calligrapher. Very sensible, but distinctive. There are 27 horses listed and no misspellings. Counterfeitcash. Key Measurements. Counter Espionage.

Flat, nasal results of the eighth race at Aqueduct echo through the room. I cannot see the loudspeaker anywhere. There is no static. I wonder how the results are transmitted from New York.

Mister Rogers moves quickly to the Aqueduct board, head cocked to listen. With the flat of the chalk he draws 1, 2 and 3 on the winning entries. He letters the payoffs in dollars at the top of the board. School-perfect numbers. Firm hand. No mistakes.

He is (I am told) Roberto Acosta Cuerva. The Frog Man.

I wave my hand to catch his eye. He steps down

from the ramp to talk to me.

Yes, he is Acosta. Yes, he is the one who paints the rocks. No, he has never been interviewed before. Not even by the papers here in Ensenada, where he lives. Yes, he would be willing to talk about his art. And about ideas. Under his arm he carries a book which he has apparently been reading during breaks in the day. He holds the book up momentarily. "Do you like philosophy?" he says.

I can tell that Acosta is not a funny man.

He appears serene. He is a pleasant fellow, casually interested in the interview, but more as an experience, I gather, than as a benefit to him. Acosta, I think, does not give a fig about publicity. But he will always talk, he says, about ideas. Particularly if they make a modicum of sense. Plato, Borges, and Sagan are in his ballpark, I deduce after some conversation. The Three Stooges are not. These days Acosta is fascinated with the New-Wave Humanism, and he tries to help me to understand a few passages from the well-thumbed volume at hand. It is a Spanish edition of Dan Custer's *The Mind in Human Relations*, which, he says, has helped him considerably in feeling more complete in his relationships with others. Custer is from Philadelphia, Acosta says as he lays the book on the table between us, and is doing some very fine work in defining humanistic principles.

I make a note to go to the library.

Acosta's range of knowledge is matched by his expressions. The face is sensitive, mobile. I find myself waiting for another emotion to be betrayed.

128

A new shift in mood.

Acosta is 47. He has five children. Three boys and two girls, 23 to 14. He enumerates from oldest to youngest and remembers all their ages without hesitating. He loves them. They are very important to him. I can tell he has mentally left the room and is gazing at his children in his mind's eye.

He hawked peanuts at Caliente Race Track when he was seven. His father, Manuel Acosta, was one of the pioneers of the track. "Do you know Johnny Alessio?" he says. He smiles fondly. (Alessio is the San Diego businessman who operated the track for many years.)

When he was old enough, Acosta went to the secondary school held in the old casino at Caliente. "It was a semi-military school. Very good. It is still in existence."

In the mid-1950s he went on to technology school in Guadalajara, but he did not like math and he was "poor with words." He was interested in the arts, medicine, politics, philosophy. In 1955 he transferred to the *Escuela de Artes Plasticas* in Mexico City. He thinks Cuevas is Mexico's greatest artist, but feels Mexican art has suffered with the loss of the epic muralists and the lack of a fiery search for *libertad* in the new art.

"Yes, it would have been nice to become a fine artist. Professionally. A wonderful life. Very satisfying. But there is the matter of practicality. One must think of the family. Of food for the children. One artist in a thousand is good enough to become truly

129

sustaining. It is very difficult. Very risky. I worked with my brother for awhile in Tijuana. We made ceramic tiles and sold them to the missions in Alta California. San Luis Obispo and others. But I could not make a go of it. My brother is a dentist now. In Tijuana. I went to work in the painting department at Caliente for 15 years.

"But I always loved Ensenada. I loved the countryside. I had dreams that the track would move to Ensenada and my job would be here. Then the Foreign Book opened here in 1972 and we moved down.

"I love to hunt. Especially quail. But, of course, other birds as well. Ducks? Yes, ducks too. And I got a mountain lion near here. You know. A puma. The puma is a wild creature. Very elusive. Very difficult to hunt. I love hunting and being out in the wild. I work six days a week in this room. Of course, on Sundays I drive a lot in the country with my family. I don't hunt as much as I used to. Walking the ramp all day has ruined my legs.

"You wonder about the rocks that I paint? Do people think I am crazy? Oh, no. I don't think anyone thinks I am crazy. People like art they can understand. Simple things. Things that come from nature. Frogs. Birds. Other animals. No one questions why I paint the rocks. They know why I do it. I do it because I must do it. I suppose it is — how do you say? — an *obsession*. We all have little obsessions of one kind or another. Is painting rocks so strange if it makes people happy?

"All the time, people come to me with photographs they have taken of my rocks. 'It is wonderful,' they say, of this rock or that. Of course, I am pleased that they like the work and find joy in it.

"I started with the small frog near Bajamar about seven years ago. I used to pass that rock all the time. The frog was very clear in my imagination. Then I thought of all the people who would pass that rock and never see the frog. I knew they would enjoy it if only they could see it. All I did was add paint to the rock. I made the frog clear to them.

"I guess the frog is very famous now. People come to Ensenada all the time and ask who painted the frog."

The Bajamar frog seems to get a new coat of paint every once in a while. How often does Acosta have to do this?

"Oh, I don't do it," Acosta says. "A lot of my work is repainted. You know. Kept in good condition. A lot of different people do it, I think. Who are they? You never know. The rocks belong to everybody." He shrugs.

"It is easy to find all kinds of objects in these rocks," he says. "Have you seen my *calavera* at Piedras Gordas? The skull? It is near my big frog on the road to Ojos Negros. A very large rock on the curve in the road. Everyone calls that place *Curva Calavera* now. I haven't finished the skull yet. The top is not finished. The top is hard to reach. The rock is very large. Five years I have been working on that *calavera*. Oh, well, some day. *Poco a poco.*

"My best work? Oh, I don't know. My big Piedras Gordas frog is probably the most famous. People stop to take pictures of it all the time to show their friends. I saw that frog for 15 years before I finally did it. But, you know, I always had little children with me. I could not stop and paint for three or four hours. Finally I just had to go up there and do it. It is a very big frog. I think it is quite good.

"But I have done many other things. Many smaller rocks. Some, like the head of the panther on the road to Agua Caliente, have been washed away by the rains. Disappeared. I have a good Virgin of Guadalupe at Piedras Gordas, near the frog. A big one. And there is a *lobo marino* (sea lion) at Laguna Hansen. There is another rock there, too. An airplane. About a mile before you get to the lake."

Suddenly, a wave of sadness.

"Oh, there is so much to do. So many jobs. But there is the matter of time. And paint is so expensive. But I must do them, of course."

The loudspeaker drones some more race results. Acosta says, "Forgive me," and moves quickly to the ramp, marking the winners in the second at Hollywood Park and (on one of the boards that is still very wet) listing some more horses' names, though the chalk marks are barely visible on the wet board. When he returns, he is pensive.

"There are the sea lions and the bear..." he begins, then stops, seeing that I am confused.

"I'm sorry," he says. "Of course, you haven't seen them yet. These are things I have to do. New work.

The new sea lions are near El Mirador. There are two together. A large one and a small one. They are very clearly there. It is private land, though. I suppose I will have to get permission. And there is a big white bear as you pass the bridge near Bajamar. It is covered with geraniums right now, so I don't think anyone else can see it. But it is there. And there is a quail, a fine quail, near Allecitos on the road to Bahia de las Palmas."

Acosta's eyes flash with excitement. "Ahh, and the Virgin!" he says. "Wait until you see the *Virgen de la Bahia de las Palmas!* She is perfect. A very large Virgin, you know. With her robes held out like this. She is beautiful. It's going to be one of the best. She is in the cemetery there. She is waiting for me. I need maybe two days and a lot of paint." The face darkens again. "It will take me maybe a month going back and forth. And paint. Paint is so expensive."

Considering the high price of paint in Mexico, I quickly calculate that the cost for such a project could amount to two weeks' salary for the average Mexican.

Is Acosta religious?

"Religious? No, I don't think you could say I am religious in the everyday sense. I don't go to church. There are many who go to church whom I would not call religious. They think themselves to be religious, of course. No. I believe we will be judged by our acts, not by our thoughts. Have you read much Og Mandino?"

I search my memory. Acosta moves mercifully on.

"Og Mandino. He is a popular modern philosopher. Good living through actions. He has a famous book. Sold all over the world. *The Greatest Miracle in the World.* It is printed in many languages."

Acosta, I see, is disappointed in me. No. Not disappointed. Sorry.

"Religion?" he says. "I study religion, of course, but it is not of prime importance to me. Let me tell you a story."

(Acosta then told me of an incident in his personal life which most men would find it difficult to reveal to the filigreed grille of the most sacrosanct confessional. It was very painful for him. The face was tortured. Like a dark, thorned Christ from El Greco. Tears rose. We had spoken together for only an hour, yet the man's soul lay on the table between us. When I couldn't take any more, I stopped him.)

"I have noticed something on the tote boards," I said, "that I would like you to explain to me."

I said this fully realizing the shallowness of the remark.

He knew.

"There," I said, pointing at the tote, "where you have written the names of horses on the board that is still wet. The names are nearly invisible. I can barely make them out. How will anyone read them?"

He smiled.

"The chalk makes its mark," he said. "The names are all there. Soon the board will dry. The chalk will dry. You will see the names. They will become very clear to everyone in the end."

AMOK IN A
MEXICAN BAKERY

Operating on my motto "Nothing exceeds like excess," I have been occasionally known to "overdo" in the food and grog department. My friends will slap their thighs and guffaw at that line, noting it as possibly the understatement of the year. But you have to remember that I was a Depression kid. We ate anything put on the table, and as much of it as we could. I was a cheap kid to feed, though. For a while we lived in a little upstate New York farm town while my dad looked for work in the city. I was absolutely goofy over dandelion greens, which I used to procure by digging dandelion divots out of the ninth fairway at the local golf course. The groundskeeper and I were mortal enemies, and more than once I would look over my shoulder as I fled with my bag of greens, to see him furiously shaking a Byron Nelson niblick at me.

I don't know what the hell there was in boiled dandelion greens that my scrawny little body screamed for but whatever it was the very same chemical or substance or *something* is apparently found in great quantities in the Mexican cakes and pastries called *pan dulce*.

I have vague hopes of some day isolating the mysteriously addictive molecule and injecting it into a wide assortment of low-calorie foods in which I am currently disinterested.

In the meantime, I am into *pan dulce*.

As a result, I now buy my suits at California Tent and Awning Company and I have to use the truck scales at Ensenada to get an accurate reading of my avoirdupois.

My *pan dulce* supplier is a guy named Feliciano who operates a dynamite bakery called "*La Panaderia del Valle*" at the south end of Maneadero.

The shop used to be on the main drag, but about six months ago Feliciano moved to another location. That was a terrible day for me because I had no idea he was relocating. I skidded to a halt in front of the shell of his old building and stared in disbelief at the sign in the window.

It simply said "moved."

It did not say why, where, when, or whatever.

Just "moved."

I immediately experienced the first early shivers

136

of withdrawal and drove like a madman to a grocery store down the street to see if the proprietor knew Feliciano's new turf.

The grocer, who is aware of my habit, detected my anguish instantly when he noticed my thumb in my mouth and my security blanket trailing behind me.

"The bakery moved to the street next to Immigration," he said quickly and with some sympathy. "Everybody in the village knows. We thought you would know, too." He shot a glance at his wife and they both shook their heads sorrowfully at my condition.

Minutes later I lurched into Feliciano's spanking new bakery and dove headlong for a pineapple torte, scattering glazed doughnuts like bowling pins.

I ate till my little cheeks ballooned out like a squirrel's.

"Ahh, señor," Feliciano's wife grinned, "you found us! How do you like the new place?"

"Ifth berry nyfthe," I responded. "Werth Felithiano?"

Her reply set off skyrockets in my brain.

"He is making *vudin*,"* she said, eyes atwinkle.

Now, for those of you who do not know, *vudin* is a molasses layer cake that is 100% calories, all of

---

* From the Spanish *budin* (pudding).
This is one of many Baja words one will not learn in Spanish 1-2. I particularly like *lonche* (lunch), *yonke* (junk), and *hamburguesa*.

which are of the type nutritionists refer to as "empty," i.e., upon ingestion they turn immediately into enormous globules of fat in the *gluteus maximus* and the lower abdominal regions. *Vudin* is not light and fluffy like your pantywaist Betty Crocker stuff. It is rich and exceptionally heavy. In fact, curiously, *vudin* has exactly the same specific gravity as moon rocks, so it doesn't take much to totally pig out on it.

Suddenly Feliciano appeared from the back room bearing a king-sized tray of the insidious stuff.

"Ahh, señor Fred," he simpered, a wicked look on his face, "you are just in time for your favorite. *Vudin.*"

I don't remember much after that. By the time my blood sugar approached normal again, three days had passed and my wife found me in my Archie Bunker chair, staring blankly out the window and mumbling something about Mayan chocolate eclairs.

If, as a visitor, you have passed through Baja without getting a bakery fix, you have missed the quintessence of the place.

Hang around a Baja bakery long enough and you will not only reach caloric nirvana, you will know who is sleeping with whom, how the fish are biting, and the price of avocados.

In many Baja villages which are not blessed with a comfortable community plaza, the bakery and the barbershop are like big-city newsrooms.

138

And the bakery is a good place to see Baja as it really is.

Local bakery items, for example, offer a clear reflection of the strange, incongruous cosmopolitanism of Baja's at-first-glance homogeneous and insular people.

In nearly every large Baja bakery, one will find small German-style strudels, English cakes, Chinese almond cookies, flaky French pastries and croissants and always the roll-sized French loaves called "*bolillos*," which have become second only to tortillas as the national bread of Mexico.

While not large by city standards, Feliciano's place is probably typical of Baja's village bakeries. He riseth early in the morning and puts in a crunching work day, six days a week.

Feliciano now has a family of eight, I believe. He has learned his Number One lesson perhaps too well, though he is inordinately proud of his accomplishment. His wife Estella and all the little Felicianos old enough to walk are all part of the bakery act.

The couple has one little girl (whom I suspect of prepubescent genius) who can calculate change in either currency and from one currency to the other, to the centavo, despite rapid-fire peso devaluations which constantly distract and which leave the child's elders in a miasma of fiduciary hysteria.

There is a reverse-sexist division of labor in Feliciano's operation, with Estella and the girls handling the front office and Feliciano and the older boys

139

whomping dough.

The family is better off than most residents of their village due to this family effort and the nature of their business.

Bread and beans are the very last items cut from the Mexican budget, and while Feliciano's prices are ridiculously low compared to a gringo baker's — here, ingredients are subsidized by the Mexican Government — Feliciano does okay by virtue of volume. He is a good baker. And his product is always in demand.

(I am reminded of the prosperous little haberdasher on New York's Second Avenue whose reason for success was gilt-lettered on his front window — "Ya gotta wear pants.")

The bakery is attached by an open patio (filled with big fluffy geraniums, a three-legged Kenmore washing machine and a parrot who sings *La Cucaracha*) to a three-bedroom stucco house from which Mexican music seems perpetually to emanate. I deduce that the radio was poured in with the foundation, and while the speaker has remained exposed, the volume control has apparently not.

There is a dog or cat in every window of the house, and Estella's white-haired mother, happily calling to her grandchildren, is frozen in time and space at the front door.

There is a very strong sense of continuity in Feliciano's home.

His working area is a thirty-foot-square room at the back of the bakery building. There are several

140

large tables for kneading dough, upon which are arranged row upon row of bread and pastry chrysalises in a variety of shapes. Later, with long wooden paddles, these will be slipped into the brick-lined, diesel-fired ovens at the back. One smells yeast, though it is technically odorless, and feels the heat. There are jars of raisins, pineapple filling, fig jam and apricot jam, and bulging white cotton sacks imprinted *harina* (flour) and *azucar* (sugar). The place is spotless, though never inspected by the health bureaucracy. Neither does the IRS stand near saying, "Throw down the box." (In Mexico, the establishment cannot yet afford an army of tax snoops. In a masterpiece of solicitousness, the government's ad slogan about *impuestos* is "Pay your taxes. It's good for you.")

In the small shop in the front, racks of cookies, cakes and filled delights are arranged inside the windows for easy viewing from the bumpy dirt road out front. In one corner is the *bolillo* box, where the five-inch loaves can be gathered hot to the touch at seven and five. I don't know when the hell Feliciano sleeps.

Feliciano's *bolillos* disappear too quickly to require commonly used cinnamon-tasting preservatives. One helps oneself, using sugar tongs and a metal tray from the stack on the counter.

The tongs, I have found, make excellent percussive whatchamacallits, and I often do a clattery fandango after sampling the big sugar cookies with the cherry in the middle.

141

It amuses the children, and I feel okay about it.
A tip:

A trip to Feliciano's is always an adventure in exercising one's power of choice, but if one gets to the bakery on a Tuesday, one might find Feliciano making *vudin*, which contains oodles of a substance found also in dandelion greens and which, I suspect, originated someplace in North Siberia where it was baked, put out to cool, and later used for making very sweet, hallucinogenic hockey pucks.

MAÑANA

"Jim Ruch, staff man for Secretary of the Interior Rogers Morton, long ago straightened me out about the meaning of the word *mañana*. He told me about a workman on his mother's ranch near La Paz, whom he had berated for stalling several weeks on a job. Each day the workman told him *'mañana.'* As Jim's ire rose, the workman smiled and nodded sagaciously. 'You know, *Señor* Ruch,' the unperturbed Mexican offered, 'we have finally figured out what is wrong with your gringos. You think *mañana* means *tomorrow*. It does *not* mean tomorrow. It means *not today*.'"

— The author, *Oceans* magazine, 1973

I have always been dazzled by the colored lights and heart-stopping showbiz of the circus.

Earlier, of course, part of the joy was getting mustard on my sunsuit and cotton candy all over

Father's trousers, but over the years I have developed a keener appreciation of the genre.

There is nothing in the entertainment world like a Mexican circus. Nothing. It goes back in time to the travelling shows of America in the 1800s and the Gypsy-like caravans which to this day (though in lesser numbers) crisscross Europe and Asia, but the Latin touch of amateurish spontaneity adds immeasurably to the form.

The Mexican orchestra, which usually consists of local musicians from the village, is often frantic in its efforts to evoke excitement, and the cacaphony is often more hilarious than the clowns. Instrumentation is haphazard, of course. A snare drum or a clarinet may simply not be available in the village, but traps and trumpets nearly always are. Arrangements seem more innovative even than those of that madcap of the '40s in America, Spike Jones, who made a fortune substituting kazoos for French horns.

Most of the acts are executed by European performers on vacation or down on their luck, and they grouse constantly about the imprecision and lackadaisical attitude of their Mexican associates, sometimes berating a Mexican roustabout in the middle of an act.

Like European shows, the emphasis is on the animal acts — the cats, the dancing bear, the horses and the seals. These are nearly *always* European presentations. The Mexicans do not seem to get along well with animals. (Consider the *bull*.)

144

More often than not, the clowns are Mexican *duendes* (dwarves) and are outrageously funny. Mexicans take great stock in (and are good at) humor.

And to save money, acts often "double up." The fire eater may be seen, later in the show, on the high wire.

There is always a festival air about a Mexican circus that is a little deeper than our own. It is more childlike and more for children. Gamins, because of a *laissez faire* attitude on the part of the management, traffic almost freely under the tent walls, and relieve themselves casually on the pegs.

Animals may be seen being exercised nearly anywhere on the circus grounds before or after the show, and many parents while away happy hours with their children in the separate-tent menagerie.

I am not alone in my addiction to Mexican circuses. I have spotted bank presidents, doctors and a noted judge (all San Diegans) taking in the Tijuana editions of the major Mexican circuses. They were, strangely, each by themselves, and seemed chagrined that I had caught them. It is a sort of a closet thing.

Some are less embarrassed by the weakness.

Craig Noel, nationally respected director of the $6½ million Old Globe Theater complex in San Diego, quite freely admits his enthrallment. "It is theater history at our doorstep," he advises me of the Mexican circus phenomenon, and we have a solemn oath to do the opening of *Atayde* in Mazatlan next year.

145

Circo Atayde is the oldest among many travelling circuses in Mexico and is replete with a full complement of lions, tigers and elephants. Unfortunately, Atayde animals are not always fed as well as the pampered pachyderms and the big cats of Barnum and Bailey. As a result they tend to be more irritable.

Over cocktails, my wife and I once interviewed some circus people in the house trailer of Atayde's lion tamer, discussing this very fact.

The lion tamer (whom I shall call Hans Hoechst) professed to be a Hohenzollern captured by Gypsies as a child, then left abandoned in the tiger-infested jungles of India.

Later, he said, he wandered aimlessly across the steppes of Russia, toured with a troupe of Maltese acrobats, and piloted a Luftwaffe Stuka before being wounded and joining a Turkish circus.

It was a practiced tale, well told. Suspiciously convincing.

Hoechst was a Colonel Klink look-alike, but he was no dummy. He spoke knowledgeably of Nixon, Willy Brandt, Rilke, Haydn, the chauvinism of the French and the efficacy of feeding wild burros to his lions.

In the midst of the conversation, I was suddenly knocked off my chair by what I immediately deemed to be an earthquake, but as dishes clattered in the cupboards, the lion tamer sprang to the trailer door shouting select Deutsch curses at three elephants which were now methodically rocking the trailer in a clear cut attempt to knock it over.

The trumpeting of a big bull blasted through the tiny window in back of me, and looking up from my position on the floor I saw Syl swaying with the motion, her eyes flashing with terror.

From somewhere the German produced a stick, bolted out the trailer door and started swinging, scattering the trio like bowling pins. "Raus, Pedro!" he screamed at the biggest of the three, which was still dragging the chain and peg with which it had been tethered. "*Raus! Raus! Raus!*"

In his spangled pants, with suspenders hanging loose at his sides, the animal expert thrust repeatedly at the rump of the rogue bull until the old boy ambled off, his coterie of tubby damosels drifting along behind him.

Then the bull stopped short. In the dim orange arc light of a single pole lamp, his trunk searched out a rumpled shirt on the ground, and the tropical stillness of the deserted circus grounds was suddenly rent by a primordial cry of such anger and intensity that it snapped all of us back to our original state of shock.

We gazed saucer-eyed at the next act.

First, the enraged bull repeatedly slapped the shirt hard in the dirt, raising eerie clouds of dust which seemed to glow from within as they rose toward the solitary light. Then, with the big top looming behind in the semi-darkness, the three elephants began to sway simultaneously in mystical rhythm, their trunks raised skyward like giant cobras moving to some unheard flute.

One by one, the great beasts trampled the shirt into the dusty midway. It was transparent that the owner of the shirt was being brutally flattened in effigy.

When the animals had completed this part of the ritual dance, the big fellow picked up the shirt once again and tossed it high into the air with an ear-splitting trumpet.

A second trunk caught the garment as it fell, sending it quickly upward again, its ghostly arms, lit by the pole light, flailing against the black sky. This went on for some minutes.

By now, there were a dozen roustabouts surrounding the ponderous executioners, but it was the elephant trainer himself, a tawny Egyptian moving purposefully with a short baton, who finally herded the elephants back into their enclosure where they were again pegged to the ground.

Hoechst and the Egyptian were furious.

The animals' watertubs were empty.

The guilty roustabout's shirt lay crumpled, but unbloodied, in the dust. When questioned, its owner (a frail little fellow, weaving with the effects of his after-hours tequila) whined aloud about the inequities of a job that cut into his own drinking time.

The German returned to his trailer in dismay.

"*Mañana, mañana*. Vun vould zink zey vould be more careful about filling zer tubs," he said distractedly, finally settling back down to a fresh cocktail. "Zose elephants killed a little boy in zer streets of

148

Mazatlan last week."

Then, with an accommodating smile: "Now. Vat vould you like to know about zer Mexican zircus?"

Is the incident *ha-ha*? Hardly.
But it is *pura Baja*.
I felt that after meeting class acts like the Frog Man and Feliciano the baker, you should see one of the warts on old-hooker Baja before you start getting starry eyed.

One of my editors, a bright young man with a fine command of the language and a keen sense of balance, quite reasonably insisted that I leave the above episode out of this account. "It has no place in the book," he said. "It is a terribly sad incident. If you want to introduce a German character, at least make it a German character who is *funny*."

He is absolutely right, of course.

THE HAMBURGER THAT
GOBBLED

Helga Von Kammer.

I haven't seen her around for awhile, but *ach*, vat memories dot name inshpires!

Helga is the most intimidating *liebschen* it has ever been my misfortune to encounter, but she makes up for it with yuks.

She arrived at Campo Loco about a decade ago and took the camp by storm.

Helga was about six feet tall, built like an NFL tackle, and had a voice that would fracture a nail.

A Brünnhilde with muscles.

In her dangerous late forties, she was (we would often be reminded) from Hamburg, Germany.

"I am a Hamburger," she would boast, with an imperious flashing of eyes. "Undt Hamburgers get zings done!"

Helga, it seems, was working as a financial wiz for a large bratwurst company in Los Angeles and was looking for a hideaway where she could spend some of her apparently endless supply of money, indulge a thoroughly developed and ecumenical sex drive and become the *Burgermeistress* of her own village. One got the feeling that Helga was on the lam.

Baja was a whole new ballgame for Helga, and here she saw her chance to finally realize her dreams of leadership.

She immediately made it apparent that anyone who crossed her, gringo or Mexicano, would be made to suffer, and the first thing she did when she arrived at camp was to hire a firm of attorneys from Ensenada, just to have handy.

Her second move was to trot out a gigantic bull-whip. Everyone detected her proficiency with the weapon the moment she snapped away the first beer can, and for a while bullwhip practice was a daily event.

Sensing, however, that no one in camp was going to vote her in as Burgermeistress, Helga soon changed her tactics and set out on a campaign to win friends and influence people.

She put away the whip, stopped making advances to the married men in camp and started doing good deeds.

She brought cartons of delicious bratwurst with her on her weekly trips from Los Angeles and distributed the larder throughout the neighborhood. Without asking anyone, she paid for a small fence to be built around our little group of homes to keep the grazing cows and horses out of the flower gardens. She bought Mamacita's oldest grandson, Eduardo, an old Chevy van which, in Mexico, is like buying an established practice for a kid about to enter medical school. A set of wheels for hauling, odd jobs, etc. (*servicio particular*) is a moneymaker for an enterprising Mexican youth and can lead to comparative riches.

But Helga simply could not shake the authoritarianism that was her trademark.

Helga was a Hamburger and would always be a Hamburger.

She intimidated the Mexican crew she had hired to refurbish the little house she had leased. This giant woman, swaggering around like a Marine DI, barking orders and pitching in herself when the going got tough, was a serious threat to the *machismo* of the work gang.

The woman was not an easy study for the *muchachos*, and she got little or no cooperation until she hit on a plan to mollify them.

She upped everyone's pay, served beer, bratwurst and other favors to all at regular intervals, then reveled as the hammers started to fly.

Soon, all the *muchachos* in camp wanted to work for "*El Alemaña*" — a curious admixture of masculine and feminine, meaning "the German." But the plan backfired. When the boys saw how close the casa was getting to completion, they staged a work slowdown that drove Helga into frantic rages and deep despair.

She actually cried. "Vy don't zey like me?" she blurted after one particularly slow day. "Vy don't zey vant to get der verk done undt see how good it looks?"

The head-on clash of German and Mexican spirit was pathetic, but Helga's will and determination won out, and she finally got her house finished.

I would have made book that the job would never see fruition, and that an era of permanent employment and sensual renaissance had come to our camp, but it was not to be.

When the casa was finished, Helga settled down to immerse herself in "Mexican life." She dandled babies on her knees. She browbeat her gardener's wife into cleaning up the family kitchen. And she coerced another Mexican neighbor into arranging the junk in his yard into orderly piles — carburetors here, tires there, burned-out batteries neatly stacked, etc.

She went on a one-woman campaign to bring order into the lives of half a dozen superbly contented Mexican families.

"Ve are goink to upgrade zem," she told my wife one day, with a broad wink and a little clucking sound. Sylvia walked away shaking her head.

Helga's attempts at disproving determinism were often serio-comic.

Helga was a hell of a fisherperson. She would go out with one of the Mexican boys and sit there all day peering into the water, wiggling the tip of her rod and saying very sternly, "You vill bite!" The rest of the time she would bark commands to the boatman in *Alt Deutsch*. The Mexican would smile and execute the exact opposite of each command, almost as though he understood the language.

One day I was down at the boat ramp cleaning fish when Helga showed up with two Mexican beach boys, a huge cardboard carton in her pickup and a thick manual, written in German, under her arm.

By now, Helga had learned a little Spanish, and she was shouting garbled instructions at her assistants. "*Abierta el carton mit der chingadera* for the nails. *Schnell!*"

I refuse to translate this.

Anyway, the boys started prying open the card-

154

board box with a hammer and I soon noted that what we had here was a rubber raft of German origin, terribly expensive and precisely constructed of the finest materials.

Helga opened the manual and began reading from page one.

Despite the best efforts of the beach boys, within an hour the handsome raft was inflated, a high-tech outboard motor was installed on the transom, and Helga was ready to go. Her final maneuver was to pull the inflator hose out of the valve. Then she climbed aboard.

I could not help but notice that she had failed to secure the valve with a small threaded plug which was attached by a lanyard to the valve itself, and I brashly made a comment in this regard.

Helga stepped out of the raft, stood on the ramp and leafed furiously through the manual.

"*Ach, nein*," she said, slamming the manual shut, "It iss not in zer book. Zere iss nussing about putting zer plug in zer hole. If you haff to put zer plug in zer hole, it vould be in zer book."

With that fine piece of ratiocination, she and the beachboys slid down the ways and headed for open sea.

While the boys stroked with sturdy Dunkenworter canoe paddles, made in the Black Forest, Helga stood arched on the foc'sle like Washington crossing the Delaware, hand in military salute, shading her eyes from the bright sunlight.

By this time a group of Mexicans had gathered on

155

the beach. More often than not, Helga's adventures came to extraordinary conclusions, and the locals seldom missed an opportunity to be present for the fun.

The raft did not start sinking until it was forty yards out in the water.

The beach boys made a break for it quickly, swimming expertly to shore, though nearly drowning with laughter.

Helga moved back to the helm.

She never once changed her position or took any note of the air hissing from the undocumented valve, but stared directly ahead like the Commander of the *Graf Spee* eyeballing a distant British cruiser.

It was not long before the two bulbous ends of the raft rose slowly out of the water making a lopsided V, at the center of which Helga stood rigidly, hand still to brow. She did not change this position until the vessel collapsed entirely, the bow gently folding over and coming to rest on her dazzling golden sconce with the certitude of the sun setting in the West.

Succumbing to the surety of disaster, *Kapitan* Helga bent forward ever so slightly and executed a perfect jacknife into what she anticipated to be several fathoms of water. As it happened, she was directly over a mud bar, and the Mexicans were treated to a grand moment of Germanic gymnastics as legs scissored furiously in the air.

"Vat hass happened to Cherman pride in verkmanship?" she bubbled to me, puffing up from the water's edge, a bedraggled naiad. "I ask for a raft, undt zey zend me a zubmarine!"

It was about two weeks after der sinking of der Graf Spee when Luisa Galicia, a sparrow-like little Mexican woman from down the road, ebony hair pinched in a bun, came to Helga's door clutching her black shawl, a large Tom turkey under her arm. The woman was obviously upset, Helga could tell, and keep peering through the doorway into the living room as though looking for something.

Not understanding a word Luisa was saying, Helga finally took her by the arm and hauled her down the hill, turkey and all, to our casa.

"Vat iss she sayink?" Helga demanded, holding the frightened Luisa at arm's length for me to cross-examine.

By now Luisa was desperate to flee from the Valkyrie, but managed to get the story out.

Luisa's two *wojolotes* (turkeys) had disappeared from her yard that morning and her son Paco had seen them over at the German lady's place at noon, eating the wild bird seed out of the bird feeder.

Luisa had found the Tom turkey under Helga's porch, and here he was, under her arm. But she could not find the hen. Was the German lady cooking the other turkey?

"Ach!" Helga exploded after I translated. "Vy vould I shteal her turkey? I could buy a hundred turkeys!"

This explanation did not help Luisa one bit, and

157

she glanced back at me quizzically.

"What did the German lady say?"

"She says she doesn't have your turkey, but she wants to help you find it," I fudged.

Just then, Luisa's fat little boy, Paco, came puffing through our garden gate. He had spotted the hen down in the arroyo, but it was hiding in some cactus and brambles and wouldn't come out.

I explained all this to Helga.

"Do you haff a piece of shtring?" she asked cryptically.

I nodded.

"Vell, go get it. I vill show you vat a Hamburger can do!"

As I emerged from the toolshed with the string, Helga was wrestling the Tom from Luisa.

"She's taking my other turkey," Luisa moaned, tugging at the poor bird.

"It's all right," I assured her. "The German lady is going to help you find the other *wojolote*."

Now in sole possession of the gobbler, Helga proceeded to tie the string around one of its legs. The other end she tied around her own wrist. Then she went clomping off toward the nearby arroyo like a zealous falconer, clutching the bird to her midsection, one hand wrapped around its scruffy neck for security.

Luisa was frozen in awe.

"Now she has *both* my *wojolotes*," she whimpered.

I took Luisa by the hand, and with pudgy Paco waddling along behind us I led her over to the edge of the arroyo.

There, just below us, was Helga, on her haunches, craning to see into the thicket. She still had the Tom by the throat, but was now turning its head toward her and looking directly into the beady little eyes.

Then Helga gobbled.

"Now," she said very sternly to the humiliated bird, "*you* vill gobble!"

A pitiful croak emanated from the bird's craw as Helga gave it a little shake.

"Now," she insisted, turning the bird's head and pointing it toward the thicket, "you vill gobble!"

As she let go of the strangled turkey, it fluttered to the ground with a squawk, then wobbled to its feet.

Helga rose and stood there, with the tiny string around her wrist leading to the bird at the other end, like a Park Avenue matron watering her schnauzer in Central Park.

Suddenly the Tom's feathers burst outward, then collapsed as it gave its first spastic shake of freedom.

Within a few seconds the Tom obeyed Helga's order, and from the rolling hills to the west, from the sage-covered ravine to the south, from the cactused slope upon which we stood, reverberated the most eloquent and profound gobble I have ever heard.

The hen bolted from the thicket.

Helga dove as it darted past, snatching at a leg.

The hen gave one agonized cry of capture and the day was won.

Helga rose slowly, a large, agitated bird dangling by its feet from each of her iron fists, the great wings beating against her heaving breasts.

Her shoulders were back and she tossed her head in victory as she held the captives high.

"You zee vat a Hamburger can do?" the old warrior shouted from the bottom of the ravine. "You zee?"

It is a miracle those people did not take all of Europe.

FLY NOW, PRAY LATER

Every time I go up in a flying machine I get hives. Flying around Baja has done this to me.

Of course, flying *anywhere* is a pastime one must be slightly balmy to pursue. God didn't put any ailerons on my elbows, and I haven't seen anybody else walking around with feathers poking through their jumpsuits.

But flying in Baja, especially with someone else at the controls, is particularly unnerving. Baja brings out the barnstormer in the most conservative pilots, and I always have the feeling they are going to ask me to get out and walk on a wing. They seem to lust after surprises — the incredible updrafts and downdrafts, the goats on the runway, the 80-mile-an-hour winds that come up out of nowhere.

If they could all wear scarves and goggles without appearing bananas, I'm sure they would.

If one is a serious fisherman, though, there is no better way to get to where the fish are in Baja than by air. Whether flying high over the Midriff Islands or buzzing an East Cape beach to select the ideal surf-casting spot, the vantage point from the air gives one a terrific edge over the four-wheelers blindly making their way down the dusty canyons toward untried waters.

To a fisherman it is very exciting to see fish from the air.

My friend Tom Hashimara, who gets turned on by ogling guppies in a fish bowl, nearly jumped out 'chuteless from 1,000 feet one time, clutching a fishing rod, when we spotted a couple of dozen 80-pound totuava working a beach just south of San Felipe. I swear he had one hand on the hatch handle.

But as interesting as it is, flying in Baja is nearly always tenuous. Even after several close passes, one cannot really know the condition of a landing strip until bumping to a halt at the end of it. There is no way of knowing whether there will be gas available, even at the larger strips. And the weather can change so dramatically that there is always some doubt about getting where you want to go, or returning safely.

To make matters worse, most Baja pilots have a tendency to carry more than they should (extra water, fishing gear, tools, etc.) and the terrific heat in summertime makes getting airborne far more difficult than under normal conditions.

I fly a lot with a guy named Charlie Becker. Charlie is a shade-tree mechanic who has sixteen Mercedes Benzes with geraniums growing out of them, sitting in the front yard of his ranch near San Diego. He spends a good deal of his time in Red China where he buys import items — "Snooze-alarm backscratchers and horizontal dildos," he avers, though I believe the real commodity is farm equipment.

"They're shore cute little fellers," he says of the Chinese, snapping his suspenders.

Charlie's neck is crimson.

Charlie's a big, bushy-browed guy who loves practical jokes and never seems to get serious. For some reason, one always gets the impression that he is somewhere else, perhaps thinking about a wrench he has misplaced, how he will get the grease out from under his nails, where he will make his next million. Who knows?

Charlie and the Reverend T. J. Smith used to search out ways to drive each other to the brink of googly.

One day Charlie showed up at T. J.'s cantina for a six-day poker game, wearing an expensive and distinctive new flying hat. It was a genuine Stetson, ten megameters high, with the initials "C.B." stamped in gold on the sweat band inside.

He got bragging about the hat so much that it drove T. J. to kicking his boot into the last orange crate in the bar.

"Give me the loan of fifty dollars, would ya, Hoss?" T. J. said to me when Charlie finally went

163

home after the first day, still fondling the Stetson.

Money in hand, the Reverend vaulted into his old pickup and roared off to San Diego where he purchased a Stetson exactly like Charlie's. He even had the same initials stamped in it. "C.B."

But the hat was a full size larger.

Of course, the next day, when Charlie wasn't looking, T. J. switched hats.

When good-old-boy Charlie went to put on the hat, it settled gently around his ears. He did not say a word, though. Just took it off and looked at it for a while absentmindedly, then ambled home.

The next day he was back, again wearing the Stetson, and when he folded a pair of jacks to go to the "*excusado*," T. J. took a peek at the hat on the table. Charlie had stuffed a bunch of toilet paper in the sweatband so the hat would fit.

Old T. J. just meandered back of the bar and got out the original hat, stuffed some toilet paper in the sweatband and set it gently on the table in place of the phony.

When Charlie went to leave and plopped the magic chapeau on, it sat up on top of his head like a party hat on Hussong's kudu.

Still not a word out of Charlie, and though everybody in the place was about to explode into profound disarray, they all amazingly kept their cool. Even T. J.

The next day Charlie came back and the hat fit. He had taken the toilet paper out of the sweatband.

Of course, T. J. just switched hats again, and the

whole business started over.

It was an uproarious month at T. J.'s cantina when Charlie was not around to hear the laughter.

Charlie finally broke everyone up, though.

It was August. 110 degrees.

"Warming up nicely," T. J. said.

Charlie sat at the end of the bar, gazing quizzically at the elastic Stetson.

There was dead silence in the room when he looked at T. J. and ventured morosely, "T.J., d'yall suppose it's possible for a man's head to *swell* in the summertime?"

Pandemonium reigned.

Charlie is a good enough guy, though. Fairly level-headed. And he has a lot of hours on the meter. A hell of a pilot.

So why is it? Every time we go winging around Baja, you can bet your bottom peso that somewhere along the line there will come a frightening moment when he will turn to me with a slightly mad grin and say, "Don't worry, we're gonna make it."

I *hate* this kind of assurance.

With Charlie, you never know exactly how bad things are.

One day we were getting ready to take off from El Barril on a bumpy strip that dips down toward the Gulf at an alarming angle. The takeoff looked very dicey to me, but El Barril is out in the middle of

165

nowhere and not a place where you would want to get left behind, so I had no choice but to trust in Charlie's expertise.

"Fred-boy," Charlie said in his sweetest Texas drawl, "would y'all mind takin' off your shoelaces?" Before I could ask him why, he snapped open the engine hood and started working furiously on some last-minute adjustment. I could not imagine why he needed my shoelaces, but I could see he was too busy to bother with questions, so I proceeded to pull the strings out of my Thom McCanns. He emerged a moment later, grimy-faced, with a very grave expression.

"Is it serious?" I asked nervously, nodding toward the engine.

"No, no," he shot back, switching to a twitchy grin. "I think we're gonna make it."

A simple yes or no would have sufficed.

"Well, here are my damned shoelaces," I said, thrusting them forward in a white-knuckled fist.

To my amazement, he took the laces silently, walked over to the edge of the strip, kicked a hole in the sand and buried them. He returned to the plane with no explanation.

"C'mon, let's go," he grunted, stepping up on the wing and disappearing into the cockpit.

I didn't want to disturb him during the checkout procedure, so I held in abeyance my questions about the shoelace ritual.

As we bounced along over the chuckholes toward the lapping waters of the Gulf, I could see that we were definitely not going to make it off the ground. Yet we had passed the fail-safe point of the takeoff and were committed. I hunched down in my seat and flashed on my wastrel life. Then, at the last minute, the prop bit miraculously into the hot desert air and we swooped out over the water like a diving pelican that has suddenly changed its mind. Up we shot into the cerulean Gulf sky, the powerful engine of the Bellanca thrumming to perfection.

When I finally spoke, I was astonished at the falsetto, reedy quality of my own voice. "Charlie," I managed, as he adjusted the prop, "just out of curiosity, what was the thing with the shoelaces?"

He looked at me for a long moment without the slightest hint of humor, then busied himself flicking a fingernail against an altimeter that I could see was working just fine.

His pause in answering me seemed endless.

"Well, y'see, bo-o-oy," he drawled finally, settling back in his seat for the long ride home, "we wuz ba-a-ad overweight."

THE GRINGO CURSE

For one whole year when I was a kid, I used to stay up most of the night reading Joseph Conrad or Nordhoff and Hall, then I would catch hell the next day when I insulted a megalomaniac math teacher — she thought she had the charisma of Einstein, but her classes were about as exciting as watching paint dry — by sleeping through the multiplication tables.

Getting out of bed in the morning was always a punishing exercise for me and I had a recurring Alpha-Wave dream in which I would roll out of the sheets onto a long, shiny sliding board, via which I would be transported in a matter of joyous seconds to my chair at Public School 82 on Manhattan's East Side, nestled between "Beetle Face" Joan Shuster and "Terrible Tommy" Zlotnik in what was known as "probation row" at the back of the room.

I don't know why I was in such a hurry to get to school. Beetle Face was as testy as a junk-yard dog and Tommy's idea of a good time was to see how deeply he could imbed the brassy point of an inkwell pen into my baby fat before I would let out a yelp.

I only learned much later, when studying Freud, that the sliding-board dream was probably all pre-maturation sexual fantasy, though I don't remember getting turned on by Beetle Face. I was only eight, for God's sake. I was more into comic books and penknives, as I recall. I could barely understand Conrad.

I don't think Freud knew Beetle Face anyway.

Lucky Freud.

But you see, even at that tender age I was already working on making my life easier. The sliding-board dream was typically American. It took Americans to invent the telephone, the Model A and the monitor-top refrigerator. I invented the perfect replacement for the school bus. Americans are daffy about convenience.

Native Bajans politely stifle their derision of this *Norte-Americano* characteristic, despite the fact that American tourists, with their nutty reactions to inconvenience, offer plenty of incentive to collapse in belly-wobbling laughter.

I once told the story in a magazine article somewhere about the couple I encountered some years ago in the old Santa Maria Hotel lobby in Ensenada. *She* was a corseted mountain of flab attached to a pair of miniature poodles. One could make out puffy little faces among her rippled mounds of cellulite. *He* was a twerp of a guy at the end of a third leash which, while invisible, was there nevertheless.

Mount Rushmore (the dog lady) was screaming at the clerk, one of the politest Baja ladies I have ever known.

"What do you *mean*, you don't have a room?" the woman shrieked. "If you don't have a room, why is there a *vacancy* sign outside?"

"I'm sorry, madame," the clerk responded with a valiant smile, "I am afraid that while we do have a *vacancy* sign, we cannot find the *no* sign. I will be happy, though, to get you a fine room just across the street." I felt that this was a delightful remark, quite in tune with the spirit of Baja. The dog lady did not.

"Well! We can *sue* you for this, you know," she erupted. "Mexico. Ugh!" Then she rolled her menagerie out of the place in a four-wheeled huff.

The entire night crew gathered round gleefully to watch the apparition, twisting and tugging at the leashes, drag her entourage across the street.

Mexicans are sometimes *so* polite about gringo foibles that one does not know one has goofed.

One time, when returning from a week of fishing at Bahia de Los Angeles, Sylvia and I were treated with special respect in every restaurant at which we stopped. Waiters and waitresses went out of their way to to please us, while seeming to be hiding some secret inner mirth. Those at tables near us turned always the other way, apparently to refrain from intruding on our privacy. It was when we got home

170

and I looked in the mirror that I understood the true depths of the kindness of Baja's gringo-mystified people.

I had used the last of our Chapstik just before leaving the hot and windy bay, and had borrowed some of Sylvia's most vibrant lipstick as a replacement. I forgot all about having it on my kisser and Sylvia was just mischievous enough not to remind me.

She is a quaint woman, that Sylvia.

Here I was, swaggering into these restaurants with all the affected *machismo* a real tough outdoorsman can muster, then flashing a cutesy-pie Revlon smile — a 24-carat horse's bucket. Another crazy gringo.

Much of Baja is still wilderness. Things are changing rapidly now, but even in Baja's cities one cannot expect to find all the conveniences which abound north of the border. Bajans have always been more or less laid back about this. In no big hurry. To me, Baja's dearth of plastic and commensurate abundance of natural wonders have always been among the most charming features of this breath-taking peninsula. Many gringos do not feel this way. They are the kind of people who seek out the dank familiarity of American bars in Paris and Rome in the springtime, the kind of people who snore in the back seat while someone drives them through the Alps, the kind who never see the moon rise over the green-velour-carpeted craters of Moorea because they don't want to get sand between their toes and they are too busy reading Harlequin romances in their beachfront hotel rooms.

I will never understand why they don't do their reading at home and save the air fare. Neither do Bajans, who quite rightfully tire of hearing them complain bitterly when the water jug in the hotel suite is only half full. (Or half *empty*, I suppose the type would put it.)

It still surprises me to notice how uncomfortable some *house guests* can get when informed that our casa has no telephone, that the water flows only until the *pila* (water tank) runs dry, that the nearest Seven-Eleven store is 100 miles away and that the lights sometimes fail when it rains.

I shudder when I hear them say, "How can you *live* this way?"

If they say it early on enough in their visit, I usually advise a hasty U turn, warning them (if they opt to tarry) to be careful of the eight-foot rattlers in the garden, the sabre-toothed coyotes that eat whole cows by the moonlight and the probabilities of contracting "*proctomorphia peligrosa*," a not-uncommon Baja malady which leaves one with a permanent droop of the buttocks and no toenails to speak of. When they have finally skedaddled in terror, I fall lazily into my hammock and gaze blissfully at the picture-postcard Sierra Juarez in the distance and at the legendary Islas Todos Santos — the "pirate islands," Tio Martinez used to call them — which lie mysterious and alluring just a few points off my starboard quarter. Then I pray that the water man

172

will not show up that day so I won't have to shave.

One of these poor city freaks arrived one late afternoon and refused to leave despite my most fanciful warnings, nay, adjurations.

Alfred Bitterman was his name.

Alfred was from New Yawk City (the borough of Brooklyn, to be precise), but unlike myself, Alfred really liked *living* in New Yawk City. He heard music in the clatter of trash cans in the alleys and saw sunshine in the flash of switchblades on the subway trains. Well, I will defend to the death Alfred's right to choose his poison, but when he superciliously condemned all points on the globe which do not have a full complement of subways and trash cans I had to wonder if the Lord forgot to give him the bolts for the Erector Set of his mind.

"I hoid you wuh out in duh country," Alfred gasped, surveying the sage-covered hills around us and staring at the blemish-free Pacific which is our front yard, "but dis here is ridikalus. Waddya do fuh *nerz*?"

I have not visited Brooklyn for a long time.

"Nerz?" I said.

"Yeah. You know. *Nerz*. Like bang-bang."

"Oh, you mean *noise!*" I said, and immediately launched into a colorful tale about a mythical family of noisy, rabid skunks which were busily building nests out of beer cans in the walls of our guest room. But Alfred remained determined to stay at least the night. He did not need to use the guest room, having arrived in a rented motorhome (the length of a

173

football field), and he decided to park it right near the edge of the sea cliff in front of our house, thus perfectly obliterating the hitherto-unobstructed ocean view.

Alfred had done a lot off "roughing it" in his fancy motorhome all the way across the U. S. A., but this was his first night in Baja.

"Where d'ya plug in?" he grunted, kicking the dirt for some kind of buried electrical receptor. (Alfred thinks everything west of Paramus, New Jersey, is one big government campground.) "Where's duh septic?"

Alfred's wife, Gertrude, never left the mobile Hilton. Being from Brooklyn, she had never walked on dirt before, and was not certain she would not sink in it.

"Goitrood wooden even go inta Central Pock until huh mudda tole huh da grass wuz astro toif ova concrete," Alfred shrugged.

Then he stepped into his eight-wheeled hotel to get out of the fresh air, which he complained was gagging him.

I did not see him again until sunrise.

He banged on my door.

"Cheez," he groaned, ashen-faced. "Wudda night! Goitrood's gone bananas. She's unda da bed an' won't come out. I gotta get huh outa heeya."

"My God, what happened?" I said, astonished.

"*Bandidos*," Alfred blurted. "Outlores. I hoid about 'em. I shoulda knowed. They wuz awl night tryin' ta break in. Rattled da screen daw. Rocked us back an' fort'. It was tevvible."

I could not believe what I was hearing.

I glanced over at the motorhome looking for wild-eyed *colorados* with evil moustaches, chests draped with cartridge belts.

There was nothing.

Just then, Hector, one of Pedro-the-man-who-rents-horses' most debilitated nags, stumbled out from behind the vehicle, browsed its way towards the "screen daw," slowly pivoted, and ecstatically rubbed its bony rump against the satisfying door handle, then ambled the length of the motorhome, scratching its flanks on the rivets as it went, just as it had been doing all night.

"Well," Alfred muttered contemptuously, "It *coulda* been *bandidos*. Yuh nevuh know."

Alfred then silently downed a quick cup of coffee with me before driving as fast as possible to Disneyland, where he would pay a higher price (in dollars and cents at least) to act out his fantasies, and where, I am sure, Goitrood would find substantially more solid footing to keep her from oozing with nightmarish agony into the deep and terrifying abyss of her most private fears.

THE TOYMAN

Sometimes one is able to unearth an entire *class* of characters in Baja.

Bill Burns is a type.

Bill is a squat little guy with hairy, telephone-pole arms and other work-related musculature. One could stick him under the globe in Rockefeller Center and no one would notice Atlas missing. Bill would be comfortable with the job. He is of pioneer California stock. That means that when the oxen stagger, one carries them.

Bill is always dressed in the garb of the trade he is currently pursuing, and his closets bulge with safety helmets, carpenter aprons, fence-mending gloves, steel-toed work boots, spraying masks, lineman harnesses, etc. He has seventeen assorted rawhide belts for holding various classifications of tools. He can look at the work of the most meticulous tradesman, point out the flaws, then make the corrections. "Fella shoulda done it right in the first place," he says, impatient with incompetence.

Bill is what is affectionately known by many of us gringos who have retired in Baja or who weekend there as a "toyman."

A toyman is a compulsive sort of Baja freak who collects vehicles and gadgets he can fiddle with in the 690-mile-long playpen called Baja, in the air surrounding it and in its adjacent seas.

Under the heading of "toys" comes a wide variety of four-wheel-drive vehicles, dune buggies, motorcycles, boats, airplanes, gliders, surfing and diving equipment, power tools, camping stuff, etc. — anything that will enhance the quality of life-after-the-freeways.

Being a good toyman is no laughing matter.

It takes lots and lots of money to be a thoroughly equipped toyman.

The really great toymen like Bill Burns get their calling early in life, sensing, I suppose, their ultimate Baja destiny. Except when they are working at their jobs (which are always incidental to their real purpose in life, i.e., being toymen) they are constantly making preparations and acquiring more and more toys for the final move to Baja, though that may be as much as 20 or 30 years away. Toymen are like goddam lemmings about finally going to Baja.

Like good soldiers with their guns, good toymen learn to dismantle all their toys and put them back together blindfolded, which they spend a good deal of their time doing. Burns' workshop looks like Willow Run, B.J. (Before Japan), and he tinkers around in there at all hours. The place is a jumble of air compressors, table saws, drill presses, lathes, routers, band saws, polishers, grinders, machines for making machines, and tool-buried work benches. 1600 labeled drawers hold 1,432,693 assorted nuts, bolts and screws.

As a class, toymen over the years become superb mechanics, machinists, inventors, carpenters, cooks, fishermen, hunters, divers and seamen. Jacks of all trades. Totally self-sufficient survivors.

All toymen have a terrifically exaggerated idea of Baja as being a total wilderness in which they must be prepared for any eventuality. Burns denies the existence of resident Baja mechanics, parts shops, grocery stores, etc., and usually returns from frequent trips to the U.S.A. stocked as though heading for an assault on Everest.

Politically, toymen rank generally from mildly conservative to outright redneck. Some are just right of Ghengis Khan. There are few liberal toymen. Burns thinks Reagan is a socialist.

With Bill, "survival of the fittest" is a transitive verb. Through it all, though, the guy is lovable in the same way one feels for A. Bunker. He is not essentially a mean man.

Most toymen do not speak Spanish. The only reason they would ever need to know Spanish would be to ask for help, and they have taken every precaution to avoid that possibility. Burns does not ask for help. He gives help. That is what he has spent his life preparing for. In fact, he can usually be found fixing a local farmer's tractor, repairing the school bus or distributing new gimmick fishing lures to the Mexicans.

Toymen are bananas about power equipment. The object of a toyman's life is to never lift a finger, but to own some power tool or machine that will do what is required. I have seen Bill Burns use a forklift to carry a 20-pound sack of charcoal to the barbecue, and all his vehicles are equipped with power winches designed to uproot sequoias.

Bill's favorite word is "torque."

Bill would never think of cutting even the smallest piece of wood with a handsaw. He would rather spend all day looking for a 7" Skilsaw (which, unbeknownst to him, has probably been borrowed by an un-toyman neighbor).

Toymen are sitting ducks for un-toymen who have no tools or equipment of their own, and unless a toyman is very careful about lending things, he will soon become an un-toyman himself.

Burns reads *Mother Earth News*, *Popular Mechanics*, all fishing and hunting publications and every book he can find about Baja. He sends for brochures about wind power, diesel motors, solar equipment and gimmicks. He has up-to-date catalogs from every major fishing tackle manufacturer and boat builder.

There is a classic debate among toymen about the ideal Baja boat and the ideal Baja vehicle. Some say a Baja boat should be small enough to launch through the surf and carry atop a vehicle. Others say the boat should be large enough to handle heavy seas and carry a lot of people and fish. Toyman A says a Baja land vehicle should be large enough to carry lots of gear and serve as a home away from home. Toyman B scoffs at this concept, saying such a vehicle is impractical on Baja's rough and narrow roads, uneconomical and altogether too cumbersome.

The real first-class toyman simply buys one of everything in every conceivable category.

Bill has an acre lot jammed with kayaks, rafts, runabouts, Ski-doos, whaleboats, cycles, jeeps, assorted earth movers, a half-track and a Cadillac. He also owns a king-sized Greyhound bus fitted out with a bar, water bed, color TV, three microwave ovens, a trash compactor and "a little wind-catching thing" that whirls around on top. While he cannot pronounce "anemometer," he knows what it is for.

Now, there are also pseudo-toymen.

These are guys with many, many bucks who decide at some point in their lives that they are going to "do" Baja. They retire on the spur of the moment without preparing for it or giving any real thought to it. They are at the mercy of RV salesmen, boat peddlers, tackle clerks and wild-eyed camp outfitters who know little or nothing about Baja and couldn't care less. These pseudo-toymen spend all of their time in Baja whining, throwing faulty equipment over the side of a worthless boat, moaning about the inadequacy of their vehicles and generally displaying all the symptoms of buyer's remorse.

If they are rich enough, after about one year they

sell or destroy everything and start over, the second time around buying the kind of gear they see Bill Burns using — the heavy-duty, commercial model of *everything*.

Toymen are terribly misunderstood. They do not buy their toys to show off. They buy them to play with. Some toymen have spent their entire lives accumulating the junk and literally have nothing else to show for it. Some toymen, except for their toys, are flat broke. Some have thrown over wives, families, whole businesses to go to Baja and play with their toys. Some toymen are miserable when they realize their compulsion is totally unrealistic. Others are perfectly happy with their craziness, and they never stop buying additional toys, eventually drifting softly into senility with the cooing and gurgling happiness of a child.

I really understand toymen.

I suppose you've guessed why.

HOW BIG *WAS* THAT FISH, JOHNNY?

A very large percentage of world record fish have been taken in Baja.

Ray Cannon, Hollywood director turned author, used to get his jollies telling about old Pete Groeschel, a grizzled Baja pro who would, when he hooked a fish in the surf, run up the beach, tie the line off to the bumper of his Jeep and yell, "Drive, Maud!"

Anglers being what they are, however, the strength, size and fighting characteristics of the fish tend to become hyperextended over the years, despite the fact that Baja is one of the few places in the world where, as Ray used to say, fishermen don't need to tell lies.

What Ray failed to note is that lying about fish is pathological. There is not necessarily rhyme or reason to it. It is related to primitive instincts about the hunt. (My grandfather confided to me, only long after I had passed puberty, that he had been lying about the size of the hairy mastodons he had clubbed to death when he was a boy. The *size*, mind you, not their existence.)

Coyote has neatly circumvented the lying problem. He has his own scale. It is a large meat market number which he found in a dump in Oceanside, California. It even has a U.S. Bureau of Weights and Measures sticker on the base of it. Few notice, as I did, however, that the face of it, segmented in kilograms, is glued over an original pound-and-ounce face. Thus, everything laid upon the magic balance is automatically more than doubled in weight.

The result of this is that now Coyote has a formal list of his spurious record fish by species, each weigh-in witnessed and authenticated by at least two observers, and he is hard to beat when telling fish stories.

I, myself, have been ruined as a successful fishing liar because of a true story which I told once too often. Coyote, the Music Man and I were fishing one day in Coyote's small boat when we got into a large school of voracious five-pound bonito. One hit my lure some distance from the boat, and when I had brought it in a short distance toward me, I gave it an extra hard yank, sensing that the hook was not properly set. The lure shook loose, dropping quietly back into the water, but the fish, given such a powerful assist, came flying through the air and landed in my lap from twenty feet out. My two partners happened to glance at my fish just as it left the water, so they assumed the creature had simply taken a liking to me. I, of course, bragged incessantly later about a special "fish call" I had developed which negated the need for tackle, pointing frequently to my two fellow anglers for authentication.

My joy only lasted a couple of weeks.

I was telling the story to a particularly skeptical outdoor writer one day, having arranged for Coyote and the Music Man to be there to back me up.

I have never seen such rolling of the eyes, such tittering, such a display of unabashed denial as my companions put on while the reporter drew heavy lines through the anecdote in his notebook and walked away in disgust.

There are enough well-documented Baja fishing escapades of merit so that one does not really have to stretch the truth.

A few years back, a long-range party boat out of San Diego was thinning the fish population on one of Baja's famous offshore banks when a few of the anglers aboard got so exhausted from hauling in fifty-pound fish that they retired to the galley for a serious drinking-and-poker session. They were well into the game and pretty well anesthetized when a roar went up from the fishing platform abaft the galley. Their shipmates had hit into a school of five-foot-long, 70-pound wahoo, a fish with the muzzle of an alligator and famous for acrobatics.

One of the most inebriated of the poker players had just raked in a $30 pot when an especially savage wahoo catapulted through the galley window in a spray of shattered glass and landed gasping on the poker table.

The drunk, still stacking his chips, leaned forward and tried to focus on the spectacular dental

184

array. As the needle-sharp teeth swam into view, he gave a little shudder, then grinned sheepishly.

"You forgot to ante," he burped.

Baja's fish are big and they're tough, and they are more than many fishermen can handle. Albacore are among the toughest, and when these longfin tuna reach the fifty-pound class, one does not simply give the leash a little tug and say, "Heel."

Every year or so, someone on one of the party boats has a heart attack while wrestling with one of these wily monsters, and the larger of the species have brought more than one angler to the praying position.

Anglers from mid-America are especially impressed with the challenge these ocean creatures present and, used to bragging about encounters with two-pound trout and bass, are stunned when they are suddenly called upon to use real muscle while fishing.

One Baja skipper likes to tell about the hotshot from Missouri who boasted shamelessly, on the way out to the albacore grounds, about his prowess. He had tussled with some big 'uns, he said, had even caught a fourteen-pound muskie up in one of the Canadian lakes. Wasn't a fish alive that could outwit him or outfight him.

"Seems sort of silly," he informed the captain when he looked at the stout 40-pound test line on his rental reel. "Hell, I could pull in an elephant with this."

A few hours out in the ocean, the boat slowed to

chum up a school of hungry albacore, which started feeding just deep enough to remain out of sight.

"Here," the deckhand said to the show-me Missourian, handing him a three-inch, wriggling anchovy for bait. "Put this on your hook and throw it over the side, quick!"

The Missourian allowed as how the anchovy was "awful big for bait," but did as he was told.

The tiny anchovy swam downward, directly into the jaws of a jumbo albacore which, feeling the bite of a hook and sensing trouble, headed for the depths. The Missourian stood frozen on deck as his rod bent double and the reel, triple the size of any he had ever used, gave off a high-pitched whine while the line sizzled away before his eyes. There was no holding the fish back. The big longfin took the whole spool, 250 yards of line, despite all the grunting and groaning the novice could muster.

He was astonished when he was left holding a rod with an empty reel.

"My God," he acknowledged to the deckhand, leaning over the rail to probe the depths with his eyes, "that anchovy fights awful hard for it bein' such a little devil."

After many years of fishing in Baja and seeing what goes on, it is easier to believe the tales of a man fighting three marlin simultaneously from the flying bridge, or jumping from boat to boat to fight a single fish, or cutting the line after being towed miles out to sea by a fish one has never seen.

But I thought I had met the biggest liar of them

all recently when I was asked by the Toyman to take a friend of his fishing. The guy had never been before, the Toyman said, and was anxious to learn the angling arts.

My student turned out to be a short Japanese fellow whose name, he said amiably, was "Rook."

On the way out to the fishing grounds in my 15-footer, I revved up the outboard to twenty knots to give the little fellow a thrill, but as I did so, he incautiously scooted over and sat up on the gunwale. "You'd better sit back in the boat," I warned him. "You're liable to go overboard."

"Oh, it's okay," he said. "I got a boat. I go faster sometimes. Fastest boat in the ocean."

We-e-ell, you know. What do you say to a guy like this?

Suspecting that we were about to get into a lying contest, I decided to give him both barrels before he could get warmed up.

"Say, what business are you in?" I sortied.

"Restaurant," he said, turning his face into the wind.

"Well, now that's a coincidence," I offered. "I studied with a black hat chef, myself, at the Four Seasons in New York. Thinking of opening a little enchilada emporium right here in Campo Loco. Nothing fancy, of course."

How did he look at me?

Inscrutably, how else?

I told him of long nights in the Yukon. My career as a boxer in Patterson, New Jersey. My avocation of stunt flying.

Nothing fazed the guy.

Always the inscrutable smile.

I must admit that I got a little testy, and when he stood up momentarily to fight the biggest fish of the day, I snapped, "Look. Please sit down when you're in my boat. The only reason I am standing up is because I think I have had a little more experience than you've had. I don't want you falling overboard."

Inscrutable smile.

Later, he hefted a nice bag of fish, thanked me profusely, and went home.

I wandered over to the Toyman's casa to give a report.

"Sonofabitch kept standing up in the boat," I groused. "I had to spend more time teaching him seamanship than fishing."

Now the Toyman gave me an inscrutable smile.

Two weeks later the Toyman asked me to accompany him to San Diego's Mission Bay, where he was having a 40′ sportfisher outfitted to sit on his lot with the rest of his toys.

"C'mon," he said mysteriously, "I want to show you something."

He dragged me down the dock to an area where pennants were flying and a crowd had gathered. We pushed our way through the mob. There, just pulling away from the slip, was the longest, sleekest racing machine I have ever seen, its huge chrome-plated motors rumbling mightily.

Perched in the cockpit, helmeted and jacketed for action, was "Rook."

He waved at us and mouthed some kind of acknowledgement under the roar of the growling motors, then slowly moved off down the bay toward the sea.

"Jesus," I said to the Toyman, "Who *was* that masked man?"

I waited to hear a "Hi-yo Silver" from the rapidly disappearing "Rook."

But Rocky Aoki, owner of 47 worldwide Benihana restaurants, champion Olympic wrestler, world-famous balloonist (*Double Eagle*), skydiver, Grand Prix racer, and (that year) World Champion Ocean Speedboat Racer, just looked inscrutably ahead at the sea, face into the wind.

He is a very low key guy.

COMING OF AGE
IN BAJA

I yearn for the Polygrip concession at Campo Loco.

Not everyone here masticates with ersatz equipment, of course, but there are enough china replicas of pearly whites simmering in Efferdent every night that one could no doubt maintain a brisk trade in denture glues and cleansers without legitimate fear of seasonal layoff.

It seems to me from my view at the point-of-entry that old age is bothersome, to be sure, not only because there are no options, but because one so often realizes at this stage how inordinately long one has been a damned fool.

Don't let anyone kid you with the old saw about the wisdom of maturity and how great it must be to be old. There are just as many dumb eighty-year-olds maundering around as there are mentally lacklustered teeny boppers.

On the other hand, I maintain that a lot of what

appears to be dementia among the supra-mature — note that I did not say "the Geritol Set," as no one I know drinks Geritol, favoring either Jose Cuervo tequila or Oso Negro vodka — is not really dementia at all (in the clinical sense) but, rather, a short in the memory circuits due to overload.

My friend Buck Danvers, whose switchboard blows now and then, calls this perfidy "SCAD" — Senior Citizens' Amnesia Disease, and I suppose it is as good a sobriquet as any.

Re SCAD: I once left my casa rent payment with my then-78-year-old Mamacita Rosita during a mutual confrontation with six *caguamas* of Tecate beer, to be passed on to my landlord at the earliest opportunity. To assure that the dinero would not be misplaced or stolen, I carefully tucked the folded money under the rug in her sitting room at a point directly beneath an enclave of fruit flies which perpetually describe an invisible spiral staircase in the jasmine-scented atmosphere of that familiar setting.

As there is not so much as a larcenous valve in Mamacita's prodigious heart, I was nonplussed three months later to hear from the *patron's* secretary in Tijuana, an understanding woman name Esther, that my payment had not been made, so I hastily warped around a few sagebrush clumps over to Mamacita's casa to ask her where the money had gone

"*Se fue,*" she moaned, flashing me the Sad Indian look, "Gone. Stolen. Are you sure you gave it to me?"

"*Mais certainment!*" I burbled.

Mama does not often get carried away by my French, but she instantly grasped my meaning. I could see that she was terror stricken that the responsibility for a not-inconsiderable sum might now be hers. I took the rap and immediately handed her an equivalent amount as a replacement, but I detected that she still assumed ponderous guilt for the whole affair.

To take some of the sting out of the bee, I brutalized my old International Scout with a punishing two-mile speed trial to Luz Gomez' house for more beer. In those days, Luz' outhouse was the village liquor store, one hole being covered to the ceiling by stacked cases of Tecate in the big bottles. Fortunately for Luz, the *gendarmerie* inspected her house often, but never had to go to the bathroom while making their searches, so her illicit beer trade lasted for some years. We gringos got to calling Luz' place "Half Moon Liquor."

It was only after Mama and I had finished all the beer, rehashed the *revolución*, discussed the elusiveness of Zapata's land-reform proposals and sung an off-key duetal version of *Mi Mazatlan* that I belatedly remembered the carpet.

"Did you look under the rug?" I queried.

"Ai-eee," said Mama. "Is there not enough dirt in the world that we should seek it out beneath the *alfombra*?"

I lurched toward the imaginary X beneath the giddy fruit flies and lifted the carpet. The money, of course, was there.

Mama laughed hysterically at what she perceived to be a trick, but she was terribly relieved and we partied well into the night, capping the festivities with a hat dance at T.J.'s cantina where, before leaving, I did unintentional but irrevocable damage to Charlie Becker's new Stetson when someone actually applauded just as I was slipping into some polyneural, precision hand clapping and heel stomping close to the brim.

I could never find it in my heart to ask Mama for the return of the duplicate payment. Mama's *real* son, Eduardo, informed me the next day that his mother had found a "large sum" in her purse, was making tamales for the whole neighborhood, and was "thinking hard" about buying a used television set.

So much for Mama's memory. And house-keeping.

Memory and dentures.

Pappy O'Toole, my mining friend who makes vodka with a rattlesnake in it, has on more than one occasion lost his dentures. That is largely because he enjoys playing games with them.

We were sitting at the bar in the drive-in whore-house near El Cipres one day long ago — the roof caved in at the motel in the back and, in its final days before the whole complex was shuttered, one had to have a camper (I understand) to partake of the services — when Pappy suddenly appeared to be talking *sans* teeth.

"Where are your choppers, Pap?" I asked innocently, as a long-lashed Conchita played ineffectively with the old fraud's knee.

"Well, I don't rightly know," he pondered momentarily, then jumped off the stool in simulated pain. Reaching inside the back of his *pantalones*, he then extracted the offensive incisors, much to the delight of the dance hall girls who gathered round to commiserate. They loved the old man.

Of course, Pap would have to return the next day due to his habit of leaving the teeth on the bar (with a cigarette stuck between them) and then forgetting about them in the spirit of the evening.

I have also heard, from an inside source, of the polished old Beverly Hills gentleman who checked into Rancho La Puerta, the Baja version of the Golden Door reducing farm in Alta California. He had, it would seem, a glass eye of which he was fond (when in good humor) of dropping into his martini glass in place of the imperative olive.

One night, after tiring of four or five days of the regimen of grape cider and low calories, he surreptitiously beamed himself over to a Tecate *bistro* where he engaged in conversation with a loquacious chile rancher by the name of Obregon. Obregon, too, had the silver mantle of winter atop his noggin and a commensurate lack of what the Greeks call "*ton prepon*" (approximately, decorum) as far as his own glass eye was concerned.

The two old boys got into some fine incidental hyperbole regarding their lives with glass eyes, and before the evening was over both were downing martinis which stared back at them.

The following day, at the fat farm, a nutritionist was horrified to note at breakfast that one of her most important charges was now equipped with one brown eye and one blue. The old man was furious when he glanced in a mirror and he initially ascribed the disparity to the overabundance of fruit juice he had been asked to consume. Fortunately, a resident masseuse, familiar with local lore, knew of Sr. Obregon's ocular infirmity and, driving the company station wagon over to the Obregon rancho, made the switch despite some grumbling from Sra. Obregon. In the short time since her husband had returned from the cantina, the Señora had grown quite fond of her man's colorful change in personality, while never really noticing that his headlamps had become disharmonious.

You who are more youthful may find such irreverence for the sanctity of body parts, real or artificial, bordering on the crass, but I see no serious justification. As one's options diminish, one must glean one's laughs from new quarters, and dental and ocular games seem no more harmful to me than stuffing one's week's allowance into a PacMan slot.

One of the greatest small eras of merriment ever to sweep o'er Campo Loco was the several days following Alma Dimmick's brief joust with a toilet seat which Mr. Dimmick had therapeutically enameled in the dead of night, during an insomniacal furlough from the normally sensible pursuits of his bedtime routine.

A large, baby-blue O was welded to Mrs. Dimmick's posterior and she thought little or nothing of calling upon the aid not only of Dimmick himself, but of the maid, the gardener, her daughter-in-law and several members of her bridge club in applying sufficient lacquer thinner to the offensive letter to make its impression less severe. As a result of this episode, Mrs. D. probably has the most universally recognized derriére in Baja California Norte, yet, because of the insouciance of her age, is scarcely bothered by the fame, possibly seeing some benefit to it in the long run, when old Dimmick passes on.

WANNA BUY A DUCK?

In the last 10 years or so, Baja's famous traveling salesmen, the *fayuqueros*, have for the most part disappeared. Some modern-day Baja truck drivers, jockeying chrome-studded big-rig Kenworths, still call themselves *fayuqueros*, but they can't hold a monkey wrench to the legendary "Lobo" Guerrero and the others of his ilk who used to wobble along from ranch to ranch in their dilapidated mobile department stores, from Cabo San Lucas to Tijuana, over roads that really weren't roads at all, and who sometimes sandwiched a wad of predigested chicle between inner tube and patch to repair a puncture. I never had the misfortune of accompanying old Lobo on any of his sojourns, but I imagine that if conditions were right his cloth-treaded Goodyears blew gum bubbles as big as bowling balls.

Lobo drove a 1934 Ford truck which slowly lost its identity as parts were added from discarded Chevies, Dodges, Ford tractors and whatever other abandoned (or sometimes momentarily unattended) hulks he came upon in his desert adventures. In the early '50s, when hood ornaments were fashionable, the bonnet of Lobo's truck miraculously sprouted a child's garden of mini-statuary — rams' heads, jaguars, various birds and the stylized mugs of old Chief Pontiac and a helmeted De Soto. Lobo held that each of these, like the battle-scarred St. Christopher medal which metronomed over his dashboard, would shield him from the dangers of the road and that, collectively, they were both eye-catching and good for business.

As salesmen, *fayuqueros* like Lobo were *non pareil*. They referred to chips in new enamelware as "manufacturers' marks," and there were enough weight-producing pebbles in their kilo bags of frijoles to fracture the substantial dentures of a Massey-Ferguson steam shovel, but out in the back country the *fayuqueros* charged (and were usually paid) outrageous prices for even so mundane an item as a handful of limes, because 7-11 stores had not yet been invented.

I often wonder what my personal fortunes would have been had I opted in those early days to take out a Good Humor franchise somewhere around, say, Laguna Chapala each August, where the sand gets so hot that the lizards' throats get hoarse from screaming "whoopee."

There are still a few of the old *fayuqueros* around, but not many. One of the last (of sorts) is a friend of mine named Bolshevski. As far as I know, Bolshevski does not have any other name or names in the style of the Grandees. Just Bolshevski. And how he came by this Russki handle is a thing of great wonder to me, because he is ostensibly a Seri Indian (for business purposes, at least). Bolshevski is the sales manager for his tribe over Sonora way, though his fierce eye and unusual stature — he is a head taller than most Seris — lead me to believe that he is possibly Yaqui, or even Apache. He is a very hostile-looking injun.

Lineage notwithstanding, Bolshevski is one of the greatest peddlers it has been my fortune to observe. He puts Elmer Wheeler and the other historic teachers of the art to shame when it comes to dickerin' and the use of sophisticated sales psychology.

The stock in trade of the Seris is handcarved ironwood figurines of animals, fish and birds which Bolshevski peddles around Guaymas, Mexicali and as far south as Ensenada on the Baja peninsula. His chief market, of course, is the tourist boutiques and curio shops, but when day is done, and Bolshevski has finished calling on his list of wholesale customers, he streaks for the beaches and wherever else he can find two tourists to scrape together and hawks his woody baubles one-on-one, as it were, like Lee Iacocca huckstering Chryslers. Bolshevski loves this part of the game, for it is here that he gets a chance to hone his bargaining skills (which appear, from the start, razor-edged).

I suspect that Bolshevski could slice the whiskers off a fox by degrees while chasing the befuddled animal across the greensward. He is no less agile with recalcitrant tourists.

Like Clark Kent, Bolshevski has X-ray vision and can see (to the penny) exactly how much dinero nestles between the cigarette lighter and the house key in one's pocket or purse. He always shoots for that amount, the full bundle, no matter what the actual value of the item he is selling. How his "marks" ever scrape together the cash to get home after dealing with him is beyond me and I must presume that there are numerous flaxen-haired derelicts to this day, wandering aimlessly about Baja, juggling their ironwood figures of dolphins or ducks, wondering where their next meal is coming from and shaking their heads at their own impecunious tendencies.

Knowing my predeliction for his products (and having marked me long ago as a pushover), on his rare bad days when sales are slow and he is in my neighborhood, Bolshevski saves me for last so he can go out in a blaze of glory and get himself psyched up for the next day of peddling. Thus it was that at dusk one day he appeared at my door with a half-dozen members of his tribe, hinting for a cup of Yuban coffee, to which, I suspect, he would like to become addicted. He introduced me very formally to each of his swarthy cohorts, who were in varying degrees of authentic regional costume, including colorful Chihuahua sombreros and a skimmer from Michoacan with a superb red tassel. It did not take me long to realize that the muchachos were Bolshevski's sales trainees, and he was about to do me the honor of allowing me to become a sample customer. In short, he was about to show the boys how to get right down to a pigeon's skin without ruffling its feathers.

Fortunately, I had in my living room at the time an old pal, goes by the name of Buck Danvers, to whom I instantly redirected Bolshevski's attention. Buck is a dapper, freckle-pated, fully ripened Kansas wheat farmer of 60 who has himself done his share of bartering in his day. "I'm just a country boy," he says innocently. (The worst kind.) No one takes Buck's perfectly creased pants off in public without undoing his belt buckle. So it did not really surprise me when he whipped out a small pouch of junk finger rings and scattered a few of them on the coffee table. "I know this feller," Buck said to me with a wink. "Traded him an old Masonic ring for a dandy statue last time he was around these parts."

The Indians gathered around their *maestro*, backs to the Spanish-arched ocean view. One, who had unfortunately once made his mark as a fry cook at a McDonald's in Anaheim, chose to lie on our "sleepy couch" to watch the Saturday morning cartoons. I knew from Bolshevski's stony glance that from then on the guy was dead in the duck racket.

As Buck and Bolshevski eyed each other cautiously to plot their respective game plans, I could tell that as far as negotiating goes I was about to witness the Gods coming down from Olympus.

Like Bolshevski, Buck was a natural-born trader. And watching the two come together *mano a mano* was like observing a clash of the Titans.

Buck began the contest by putting forth his pouch full of assorted pawn-shop rings, for which he had paid prices ranging from two to ten dollars. For his part, Bolshevski lined up six handsome figurines, ranging in value from $20 to $40, graduated in size — a marlin, a ram, a porpoise, a duck, a pelican and a sea lion.

Buck poked around for three more rings in the pouch and casually placed them in a small pile in front of the statuettes.

There were two "givens" in the contest of which you should be aware. First, each gladiator really wanted, nay, lusted after the goods of the other. Seris, it seems, consider finger rings to be declarative symbols of wealth, and the more exotic the ring the better. Bolshevski wore several of them.

Buck, on the other hand, had the feeling (as I do) that the wooden figures are an excellent investment, their prices over the past several years having more than kept pace with inflation.

The other condition of combat? Bolshevski does not speak much English (as least not in matters of Seri-ous negotiation), and Buck speaks neither Spanish nor Seri. Thus, the transactions were all to be held in pantomime, with wild gesticulations, rubbery expressions of disgust or inquisition, and final-offer attitudes of crossed arms and set jaws.

If I may, I will now further mix my metaphors and move on to the heady language of chess, because from this point the match became largely an intellectual exercise, each contestant trying to outdo the other with anticipatory gambits.

Bolshevski used the classic Seri Opening (smallest figurine to Queen's Bishop 4) and Buck countered instantly with the most insignificant of his pawns (a silver-plated circlet bearing a scratched plastic imitation of a square-cut turquoise).

Bolshevski immediately pulled a "Bobby Fisher," whisked away the small woodcarving and started to leave the room in disgust. "The turquoise isn't even real," he flashed at me in Spanish on the way to the door. I suddenly realized that, for the moment at least, I had been appointed game judge.

The Kansan, seeing that he had offended the Indian, pushed a second gewgaw forward to add to the specious turquoise, this one a bulbous class ring bearing the legend "Calexico High School '63." One of the Seris in the gallery coughed on cue. Bolshevski wheeled from the doorway and returned to the table to inspect the new offering.

Now, in one of the greatest opening-game moves I have ever seen, Bolshevski suddenly snatched the Kansan's pouch of yet-to-be-revealed trading material and scattered the contents out on the table, at the same time pocketing the phony turquoise *en passant*. The daring of the maneuver flabbergasted the Kansan.

Before old Buck could regain his composure, the Indian had selected the largest of the finger bands (a Knights of Columbus number, crowned with an egg-shaped opal), thrust this ring, too, into his pocket and handed Buck the tiniest statuette, as though the bargain were a *fait accompli*.

Buck glanced at me agape, then, coming to his senses, put down the small figurine and, with boldness equal to Bolshevski's, reached for the handsomest and most imposing of the pieces, a majestic sea lion, and tucked it under his arm.

Check.

The Seri smiled and acquiesced, retrieving the opal from his pocket and replacing it in center board. Buck returned the sea lion to its proper place in the row of figures. The sparring was over. Buck wrote off the fake turquoise, still in Bolshevki's pocket. Now the dickering would begin in earnest.

The middle game was truly astonishing. In an extremely intricate series of about 50 moves, the Seri would push the figurines forward one at a time, smallest to largest, allowing Buck to counter with those of the gaudy finger-loops he felt were fair exchange for each piece. In virtually every case, Bolshevski would reach over and pull one or more additional rings from Buck's cache and look quickly for Buck's reaction to the deal *in toto*. What struck me as odd was that despite Buck's nod of approval at any given transaction no deals were actually consummated. Bolshevski would simply make mental note of all the pieces involved and then go on to the next piece of statuary, experimenting constantly with various combinations of rings and wooden figures.

Every now and then, Buck would sweep all the rings off the board, pour them back in the pouch, cross his arms and glare at the Indian. At this Bolshevski would hand Buck one of the finer carvings to examine more closely, and while Buck was checking the statue out, the Indian would snatch the pouch and scatter the rings back on the board.

The latter interruptive maneuver, intended to break Buck's rhythm, soon became a frequent ploy on the Seri's part.

It was at move 61 that I detected the total strategy of the two giants.

I remember my flash of insight keenly. On one center file were a 12th degree Masonic, a Boy Scouts of America and a somewhat impoverished silver engagement ring, at one time clustered with three scrawny garnets. One garnet was now missing. On the opposing file was a docile ironwood duck of quite nice proportions. When Bolshevski added a Mesa College '74 and a Sigma Alpha Epsilon Fraternity to Buck's three-ring offering and looked up for approval, I suddenly realized the extraordinary methodology of the whole affair.

In various past gambits, Bolshevski had tested all the rings in the pouch against one figurine or another, and in various combinations. HE NOW KNEW THE RELATIVE VALUE OF NEARLY EVERY RING IN THE POUCH. AT THE SAME

TIME, BUCK WAS GETTING A FIRM GRASP ON THE DOLLAR EQUIVALENT HE WOULD HAVE TO PAY FOR EACH FIGURINE.

Thus it was that within seconds after the penultimate 72nd move, Buck happily had the two figurines he wanted most and Bolshevski had 12 splendiferous rings, some of which he would certainly trade, when back in Sonora, for a sheep or a goat, or perhaps even the fine kerosene stove he had seen at the flea market in Guaymas. Such is the way of the Seri.

"Feller does nice work," Buck said, polishing a newly acquired duck with his sleeve.

"Him pretty good," said Bolshevski.

The other Indians sat around discussing the game like a Harvard Business School class at Gilroy's Bar after a quiz.

The human brain is surely the most intricate work of God. With all its mysterious volutes, its synapses, it enzymes and its unfathomable storage capacity for the hopes and fears of Man, it commands my greatest awe and reverence.

To have been permitted, no matter how briefly, to adjudicate two advanced models of the cerebrum doing neurogenic nipups with the ease of kids climbing apple trees was a great honor for me.

Generations from now, Baja tales being what they are, folks from Cabo to Colonia Guerrera will speak in sepulchral whispers of *"El Indio"* Bolshevski and his cranial computer, while in Wichita, even the Fundamentalists will brag shamelessly about "Trader Buck," who could skin a skunk without ever getting sprayed, and who could make the hapless animal wriggle with joy as it was being divested of its stripes.

Having these two living legends come together in my humble home in this year of our Lord nineteen and eighty-three is an event I will not soon forget.

Unto these sure and certain details of that extraordinary encounter, witnessed by me, I hereunto set my hand and seal.

MOBY DUCK

Some days one wakens at Campo Loco and one knows instinctively that all hell is about to break loose. There is something in the air. It is one of those guppy-gulping, panty-raiding, jam-into-a-phone-booth days, and there is not much one can do to avoid it unless one makes a little tent with one's bed covers, installs a new set of Evereadys in the flashlight and is fortunate enough to possess a large-print edition of the *Bounty Trilogy*.

It was high summer. The crickets were fiddling doubletime, the dogs' fleas were panting and Mamacita's rooster had hiccups.

The Ides of July.

I always know when the day is going to be especially hot. The frog under the bedroom floor stops croaking the second the sun screeches up from behind the shimmering Sierra Juarez chain in the distance.

The rap at my door was insistent, and I knew it would be useless to feign coma. My friends are of the disposition who would break in knowing full well I was nearing the climax of a whimpering death-bed confession.

This particular intruder into my recurring dream about a traveling saleslady with rhinestone garters was Buck Danvers. He looked worried.

"Hiya, sport," he said breathlessly, standing at the foot of my bed. "Better get up. We got problems."

"*You've* got problems," I mumbled, pulling a pillow over my head. "*I've* got a saleslady."

"C'mon," he persisted, shaking my foot, "T.J.'s

209

gone b'serk."

"That's T.J.'s problem," I murmured through the pillow.

"Can't hear you," Buck said, giving the piggie-who-went-to-market a special tweak.

"Okay, okay," I relented and sat up slowly, trying to rub the moss off my eyeballs.

"What's T. J. done?"

"It's what he's *about* to do," Buck puffed, handing me my *pantalones*. "Damn fool's gonna kill himself. Y'know his business has been bad all month. He's real depressed. Now he's got some crazy idea about foolin' with a whale. C'mon."

"A whale?"

"Yeah. C'mon, c'mon, c'mon."

This is the kind of cockamamy call to action from which Sylvia would normally rescue me. She would say, "Go away, Buck," and I would do a full gainer into the *Trilogy*. But Sylvia had gone home to Mother, and I was left unfettered by spousal armor.

"You'll see," was all I could get out of Buck on the way over to the cantina. "Damfool T.J. He's crazy. Gonna kill himself." That's all Buck would say.

"Ain't no sense in tryin' to talk me out of it, Hoss," T.J. said when he saw me come through the swinging doors. "Ain't no reason wha-a-ah it cain't be done."

"Why what can't be done?" I said. "What's going on?"

Charlie Becker pushed the adjustable Stetson to the back of his head and leaned back from what was

210

left of his serving of *machaca*. "Boy's gonna tra-a-ah ta rope a whale," he drawled offhandedly, reaching for a toothpick.

Pappy O'Toole, miner and rattlesnake-vodka distiller, sat across from Charlie, strumming smart figure eights on the uke.

"It's a bunch of razzamatazz," he said sleepily. "No whales this time of year. Whale migration was over in April."

"Well, Hoss," T.J. shot back at Pappy, "Ya better jes' have y'seff a look down thar at La Bocana cove, cause they's sure 'nuff one a them critters off course a mite. Been down thar all mornin' jes swimmin' roun' in the kelp." Pappy drifted off to sleep.

The doors swung open and Coyote, the mushroom king, loomed against the morning sun, carrying an armful of corn.

"When are we going?" he said, looking around at the group. "How big is the whale?"

"*Qiere menudo, Coyote?*" Anita said, routinely wiping her hands on her apron.

"Yeah, just a small bowl," Coyote responded, and went back to the kitchen to dump the corn. "How big?" he yelled.

"Ain't nobody else goin'," T.J. shouted back, opening a fresh beer. "'Sgonna be a worl' record, and ain't nobody else gonna git they name on the plaque." T.J. folded his arms and shook his head. "No *how*," he added with finality. "'Smah pawrty."

"You got a plan?" Coyote said, coming out of the kitchen carrying the bowl of menudo. "Man ought

211

to have a plan for something like that. How big is it?"

"Big 'nuff," T.J. said. "Sixty foot, I 'spect. Ain't nobody done it before, neither. Got me a boat, a *reata*'na beer keg. Gonna rope the dogie then tie her off ta the beer keg. Then I'm gonna pick up the keg an' go fer a Messican sleigh ride. Whale might take me ta China. Who knows?"

"Cute little fellers, them Chinese," Charlie said through a last mouthful of *machaca*.

Buck tapped me on the shoulder.

"Injuns used to do that back in Kansas," he said. "Rope a buff'lo, then slide for miles over the prairie grass on a piece of cardboard or sump'n. You can't *drown* in prairie grass, though." He nodded at T. J. "He's gonna get killed if we let him do it."

Just then, the Music Man belly-bumped his way through the doors and took a squeeze on the concertina. "Great idea," he said. "Just heard about it. We'll use my boat and maybe take wet suits. No use in catching cold."

"Ain't nobody else goin'," T.J. flashed. "Got mah own boat and mah own lariat. Gonna do it maseff."

Pappy woke up and strummed the uke. "Gimme a G," he said to the Music Man, bending over the uke to tune a string.

"'Smah idee. Smah plaque," T.J. reprised. "'Sgonna go rat thar over the bar. Rat next ta the telephone. 'Revern T.J. Smith done gone ta China ridin' a first class humpback jumper what he roped with a Messican reata.' A man could be real prouda that."

Charlie Becker took off the Stetson and

smoothed his hair. "Y'all think he can do it?" he asked of Coyote.

Coyote pushed away his empty menudo bowl. "Depends on how drunk he is," he announced to the group. "Too drunk, he'll miss the flukes. Probably only get one chance, then the whale'll take the deep six and head for the Bering Sea. But if he can get that rope around those flukes, good chance he can do what he wants to do. I sure wouldn't mind tryin' myself. Look good in the record book. Wouldn't want to mount the damned thing, though. Lotta blubber there. Lotta work." With Coyote's imprimatur on the project, a ripple of excitement went through the growing crowd.

Two Mexican cops were scarfing down freebie frijoles at the table near which Buck was standing.

"A whale?" one said in Spanish.

"*Si*," said the other. "With a *reata*!"

"Is his mordida paid up through the end of the month?" said the first. They both laughed.

Helga burst through the swinging doors looking like an apparition from *Captains Courageous*, completely decked out in immaculate yellow foul-weather gear, including an authentic Gloucester Sou'wester hat with the rim turned up in front like Lionel Barrymore's. She was clutching a pair of new swim fins to her bosom, along with the bullwhip.

"Vere iss it?" she said to no one in particular.

"Down in the cove at La Bocana," Buck volunteered. "It's sixty feet long. Ol' T.J.'s gonna kill himself. Don't encourage him."

213

"He doesn't haff to go," Helga said. "I vill show him vat a *Hamburger* can do!"

"Gol dang, Hoss," T.J. flashed at Helga, "that ain't ratly fair. She's mah whale, 'n ahm th' one's gonna git her."

"Vee'll zee about dot," Helga boomed. "*Menudo*, Anita! *Schnell!*"

Anita ignored the salty *oberleutnant* and pretended to be busy making *rellenos*.

"Anybody want a beer?" T. J. said loudly, reaching into the box for one for himself.

"*Si!*" the two cops sang out simultaneously.

"Guess I'll tra-a-ah one," Charlie concurred, covering a belch.

"Me an' Pap'll have one," the Music Man chimed in, starting a spirited version of *El Marinero*.

The Toyman, wearing a tilted-up welder's mask and tilesetter's knee pads, swung out of his Greyhound out front. "I hear T. J.'s gonna kill himself," he said, banging open the swinging doors. "Everybody's talking about it on the CB."

He spotted T.J. cracking another beer.

"Now look, T.J.," he began tutorially, going to the bar to draw some pictures, "the first thing you do is get that six-ton winch I got on the Jeep and rig up a set of pulleys..."

"'Smah pawrty, 'smah whale, gonna do it m'seff," said T.J., reining in the excited Toyman.

After a while, more stragglers came in from Campo Loco, anxious to find out if the whale caper was on the level. Mamacita showed. Dimmick, who was

214

yet to lose his station wagon and his mother-in-law, came by looking for a day he could rue. Bolshevski, the chess-playing *fayuquero*, had heard about the crowd and stopped by to peddle some ducks. Soon the hubbub began drawing in the desert rats, passing by in their dune buggies.

Buck greeted everyone who entered. "T.J.'s gonna rope a whale," he'd say. "Coyote says T.J. can do it. It's on the level. T.J.'s serious. Might kill himself. We really should get down there and watch him."

Before long the cantina began looking like Saturday night at Gopher Gulch, with a party of twelve college kids from Santa Barbara finally squeezing into the last available corner and agreeing to pay a head tax of two dollars apiece if T.J. would let them listen to the Music Man and bring in a green lizard (a watermelon filled with vodka and bristling with enough straws for all) from their fancy van outside.

After a while, Charlie went out to his Mercedes and got his fiddle, and the foot stompin' started.

By eleven the place was a madhouse. There were three cooks in the kitchen and Claudio-the-fisherman and Pedro-the-man-who-rents-horses slipped behind the bar and began spelling T.J. at the Margarita blendor.

At noon, T.J. bounced up on the "stage" (a 4 x 4 tractor-motor packing crate, sometimes illuminated in the evenings by two flashlights stuck in coffee cans).

"Well, now, friends," he hollered, palming the crowd to silence, "Ahma goin' now!"

The college group, which by now was also reflecting on the whale adventure, cheered lustily.

T.J. shot a glance at the farthest corner of the room, where a henhouse of astonished Dubuque schoolteachers with fat ankles and skirts to their calves, all wearing goofy-looking sombreros, were taking in their first day in Mexico.

"Any a you folks wants to go over ta La Bocana with me an' witness this hyar historic 'vent in hist'ry, why, yew jes' come rat along. The resta ya are shore welcome ta stay rat hyar an' *in*joy the moosica, 'cause the mariachis'll be hyar in about ten minutes."

"Gonna kill himself," Buck threw in for an encore.

The teachers stared open-mouthed at their host, unable to assimilate the full import of his announcements.

One of the college kids, wearing a Property-of-Athletic-Department sweatshirt, clasped his girl's hand and raised it high.

"We wanna get married!" he shouted and another cheer went up.

"Ain't the proper atmosphere, Hoss," T.J. yelled back. "Gotta wait'll sometime after siesta when things quieten down a mite. Maybe I'll perform the ceremony in the still of the evenin', after I done got mah Moby Dick."

The regulars all drank up and piled into their vehicles, the Music Man leading the procession with a rollicking *Cielito Lindo*. This made room in the cantina for a crowd of a couple of dozen more

216

partygoers who had been waiting outside to get in.

Soon the caravan was bucking and weaving over the tortuous, rock-pocked mountain road to La Bocana, 23 miles away — four Jeeps, two Broncos, a flathead-six Chevy station wagon full of Mexicans, plus a WWII weapons carrier Helga had borrowed from the Toyman for the day. Every vehicle exceeded manufacturer's load specifications by at least four revelers, not to mention musical instruments, including the squeeze box, the fiddle, the uke and a one-string washtub bass Pap always carried for emergencies. The music drifted across the hills, and by the time we arrived at the cove there were fifteen more celebrants, come to see what all the excitement was about. Twenty more spilled out of Jose Castro's cantina by the beach, and T.J., the pied piper, danced the whole contingent directly to a secluded grove of eucalyptus trees near the point, overlooking his prospective rodeo arena. Sure enough, the whale was there below us, lumbering silently among the shadowed reefs. It rose only occasionally to blow, revealing a barnacled back and inviting flukes which presented an ample target for a few opportune seconds whenever the leviathan dove again.

Somehow, Claudio-the-fisherman had arrived moments earlier with a stake truck rigged out as a bar. He was busily setting up tables and chairs and had two *La Reina* cigar boxes ready for cash transactions. The truck also bore a Casey Rents outhouse which T.J. had appropriated somewhere along the line, and Claudio duly installed it at the periphery of the trees.

Coyote arrived by way of the Toyman's garage where he had fished (out of one of the Toyman's six freezers) the results of a previous hunting expedition — 27 mallard ducks, 36 mountain quail, 71 whitewing doves and Alice B. Toklas, one of my most unfavorite rabbits. With the additional vegetables he had in the pickup, plus a dozen nice lobsters Roberto dredged up out of the cove, Coyote cooked us a picnic feast at just $4.50 a plate.

Later, Helga took the Sou'wester off and demonstrated her proficiency at the bullwhip, snapping a scruffy hand-rolled cigarette out of T.J.'s mouth, and then whipping the whole Bull Durham sack out of his shirt pocket by the tag while T.J. nonchalantly swigged his beer.

Pretty soon the whale, probably bothered by all the noise, disappeared somewhere into the deep, but few seemed to notice.

Of course, every now and then, T. J. would start off toward the trail to the cove, lariat and coiled line tucked beneath his arm, but he would inevitably get caught up in a conversation on the way, and soon he would be back shouting song requests at Roberto and Charlie Becker.

The party went on till midnight.

Biggest day T.J. ever had.

He paid Buck his $20 fee for playing a superb shill, Coyote his $50 for cooking and for corroborating to the potential audience that the whale stunt (contrary to Coyote's true judgment) was feasible, and still wound up with a combined net profit of $1754.60 for the party at the cantina and the one here on the point — enough to carry him over the upcoming Labor Day weekend and well into the winter.

With the exception of $3.88 for two jars of mayonnaise (lobster salad), Coyote threw in the victuals as a gift from God.

"Sorry, Hoss," T.J. said to me toward the end of the party. "*Real* sorry to git you up so early this mornin'. But I figgered we'd never make a day of it lessen you an' the boys come aroun' early ta prime the pump, an' it'd have t'be an all-day wingding to make enough to stay in business."

"You could have asked any one of us for the money, T.J.," I said. "We didn't know you were broke."

"Sure, Hoss, I know," he said, his shiny, sunburned face flickering with the light from the campfire. "But I don't ratly lak to be beholdin'. 'Sides, Hoss, this is *Baja!* Wha-a-ah, if'n I just *took* the money, where'd be the *haha*?"

Then he took my arm and pulled me aside to the edge of darkness. He put his arm around my shoulders.

"Fred," he said seriously, and in a strange new voice, "I just have to do things differently than most people. Guess that's why I never really fit *in* anywhere but here in Baja. Anyway, I'm sorry I pulled this stunt on you, but I hope you enjoyed the party.

Thanks for coming." At this juncture in time, I had known T.J. for twelve years, and I had never before heard him speak without the Okie-phonokie dialect.

In the end, the whole crowd straggled home, Baja happy, to dream dreams, to see visions, to assess the joy of having "wasted" an entire day amongst raving individualists, survivors like Mamacita and the others, who live funny frantic lives in a far-off fantastic land where any activity of questionable feasibility, even lassoing a whale, seems not only possible but (for some crazy reason) eminently desireable as long as there are a few laughs involved.

When I got home in the early morning hours and made my pizza, I found a St. Eusebius, a St. Melchiades, a Constantine and a Pius XII, plus an acnefaced altar boy who used to beat me up in the alley behind the rectory at St. Bridget's Church of Manhattan, then at York Avenue and 68th Street.

Strangely enough, I was in the pizza, too — a quite-accurate left profile popping out of three mushrooms, a piece of Helga's bratwurst and the tiniest little smidgeon of pepperoni.

ABOUT THE AUTHOR

Educated at Hamilton College and at New York University in Greenwich Village, Fred Hoctor has been a Miami Beach bellhop, a dishwasher, lifeguard, bartender, seaman, diver, flower peddler, horse rancher, pet cemetery manager, fishing guide, radio humorist, stage and television performer, Boston business executive, magazine editor, New York publisher, freelance copywriter, marketing consultant and creative director for a large advertising agency.

Obviously, he can't hold a job.

His travel and adventure articles have appeared in newspapers and magazines throughout the United States and Mexico.

Hoctor writes a regular column (Baja Inside Out) for the *Baja Times*, from which many of the stories in this book are taken.

He resides in San Diego and in Baja with his wife, Sylvia, who, fortunately for him, is a licensed clinical psychotherapist.